DOCTOR, DOCTOR

The arrival of a new doctor in a small Cornish hospital causes a stir, especially among the female members of staff. Lauren has worked hard to build her career, along with a protective shell to keep her emotions intact. She won't risk being hurt again, but Tom has other ideas . . . As they share the highs and lows of hospital life, they develop a mutual respect for each other's professional skills — but can there ever be more to their relationship?

CHRISSIE LOVEDAY

DOCTOR, DOCTOR

Complete and Unabridged

LINFORD
Leicester

First published in Great Britain in 2007

First Linford Edition
published 2007

Copyright © 2007 by Chrissie Loveday

British Library CIP Data

Loveday, Chrissie
    Doctor, doctor.—Large print ed.—
Linford romance library
    1. Love stories
    2. Large type books
    I. Title
    823.9'2 [F]

    ISBN 978–1–84617–945–7

Published by
F. A. Thorpe (Publishing)
Anstey, Leicestershire

Set by Words & Graphics Ltd.
Anstey, Leicestershire
Printed and bound in Great Britain by
T. J. International Ltd., Padstow, Cornwall

This book is printed on acid-free paper

The New Doctor

'That's him — look!' Jenny said in a stage whisper, nudging her colleague.

Lauren continued with her patient's treatment, ignoring the nurse.

'Sorry, I hope that didn't hurt too much.'

'No, dear. You were very gentle,' the old man said with a smile. 'You know what you're doing and I daresay it's all very necessary for a silly old fool like me.'

She spoke gently to him, explaining the procedures which would follow, and attached the drip that would soon make him feel better.

Jenny was still looking the other way, her interest anywhere but with the patient, and Lauren shook her head in mock reproval.

'So, who's the *him* you've seen?'

'New boss — by the door.'

'Keep an eye on this drip for the next few minutes, please, nurse,' Lauren instructed, smiling at Jenny. She turned to look at the object of interest and felt her heart give a jolt. The new boss had indeed arrived and she could see why her nurse had been temporarily distracted. The tall, slim man in a white coat was attracting everyone's attention, especially the females.

'Well, well. Bit of a change from Dr Matthews, I must agree,' Lauren remarked. 'Maybe Angus's sabbatical wasn't such a bad plan after all!'

'Dishy or what?'

'Jenny, you're shameless.' Lauren laughed. 'A happily-married woman like you?'

'Happily married doesn't stop anyone appreciating something nice to look at. I can see every female in the place agreeing with me.'

'You're incorrigible. However, I suppose I should go and introduce myself.'

Lauren smiled apologetically at the elderly patient and walked towards the newcomer, ignoring the nurse's grin.

'Good morning, I'm Lauren Fletcher, Registrar.' She held out her hand to the new consultant.

'Good morning, Ms Fletcher — Tom Asprey.' His eyes surveyed her thoroughly as he grasped her hand in a firm handshake.

She, in turn, took a good look at him — wavy, dark brown hair, eyes of clear blue, pleasant smile . . . Jenny was right, she thought . . .

' . . . busy?'

With a start, she realised that he'd been speaking to her — and she hadn't heard a word of what he'd said.

'S-sorry?' she stammered, flustered. 'I didn't quite catch — '.

He smiled lazily. 'It's OK. Must be the accent — New Zealand. I was just asking if you're able to show me around or are you too busy?'

Lauren glanced round the waiting room, glad of the excuse to avoid his eyes after being caught day-dreaming.

'There's nothing too urgent. Mostly

things the nurses can deal with — and the sooner you know where to find everything, the sooner you'll be able to get to work. This is usually a relatively quiet time,' she explained. 'The hoards start to pour in around ten o'clock, when the schools have got going and the G.P.s start sending on their referrals.'

'OK then. Let's take the tiki tour.'

'The what?'

'Sorry. New Zealand term. Show me around, Dr Lauren. I've heard a lot about you. Angus was full of praise for you and I've been looking forward to meeting you. I'm sorry I couldn't get here before he left the area. I gather you've managed over the weekend? Had a locum in, didn't you?'

Lauren filled him in on the weekend activities as she led him round the small, minor injuries department and explained their usual routines.

'We take in emergencies from the surrounding area, lots of farming accidents, children hurt while playing

4

on the beach, that sort of thing. Cornwall has more than its share of holiday-makers as well as being a rural community. There are also a great many elderly patients, as you'd expect in this sort of area. That's why Angus — Dr Matthews — was so keen to take up the offer of studying ageing problems. I suspect he's hoping to become a geriatric consultant eventually. We could certainly do with it here.'

'I can imagine. So what about the more serious cases?'

'They're mostly sent to Truro, which is the main hospital for the area. We do sometimes have to take more serious cases in emergencies but we have limited facilities. In life-threatening situations, it's not always possible to take them the long distance and we have to deal with it.

'But whatever, there's a vital need for this local facility to save the long journey for the patients — and their families, of course. Family visits are very necessary to help anyone get better and keep them in touch with home. There are two small operating theatres, mostly used for day-care patients needing minor operations. And we hold regular clinics, of course, for most things. The consultants come over from Truro or Plymouth for one day a week.'

'Seems like a nice set-up,' Tom remarked. His eyes darted round each room, taking in details of equipment and organisation. 'Don't you find it frustrating that the most interesting cases are dispatched elsewhere?'

'Well, occasionally, I suppose. But we really do get plenty of hands-on experience. With several wards to look after and the day-care centre, we have a wide variety of care and patient follow-up — at least, we do at the moment.'

'What do you mean by that?' he asked.

'The powers that be are always trying to find some excuse to close us down — move everything to one centre — better care and facilities. You must know the rationale.'

His eyes flared with passion at her words.

'Makes me furious. It may be easier for keeping the books straight but it does nothing for the families who have to spend half their time driving miles to visit. Big is not beautiful, in my book.'

He was going to be a useful ally, Lauren could see.

'Tell me about it,' she agreed. 'This is a country community. The folks around here don't like these huge, soulless places. The roads are narrow and most people live miles from anywhere. The older patients need their families to visit, for reassurance as much as anything. They can feel isolated in the middle of a town and especially in hospital.'

'You really care, don't you?' Tom said softly, his hand reaching out to touch hers. It was an unconscious gesture but the touch on her skin was making her heart race just a little.

★ ★ ★

Dr Asprey was an instant hit in the children's ward.

'Hello, Patrick,' he said to a small boy with a nebuliser over his mouth and nose. 'I'm Dr Tom and I'll be looking after you for a day or two. Is that special air making you feel better? I reckon you could show those spacemen a thing or two about breathing.'

The child giggled and Lauren was impressed that he'd picked up a possible interest in spacemen simply from a card sitting on the locker next to the child's bed.

He moved on to the next bed where the patient was a twelve-year-old with a much-signed cast on his leg. A quick glance at his notes and Tom was off again.

'You've hardly left a space for me to sign. I never allow a patient to leave without my signature.' He scribbled his name next to the toe. 'Good job it's only a short one. Bet you can't even read it.'

'Yes, I can,' protested the child.

'You're Dr Tom.'

'Very good. I'll see you later.'

The round went on, each child receiving his special attention for a moment or two. When they moved to the door, he looked back and waved to anyone who was watching. Several little arms were raised in response.

'It's a really friendly place,' he remarked. 'Nothing too large and frightening for them all. Great. Where next?'

'There's a very small maternity unit,' Lauren told him. 'Just a few beds in case of emergencies — babies who won't wait and home births that look like giving problems. The more difficult cases often go to Truro where they have an excellent neo-natal unit. The local midwife and health visitors are usually on the ball and come in to give us the necessary specialist help when it's needed.'

'So all in all, you get a pretty broad experience. Keeps you on your toes, I guess. I'm really looking forward to getting down to business.'

At that moment Lauren's pager beeped. She reached for the phone.

'Lauren, Dr Asprey, we need you. Ambulance coming in — ETA five minutes,' Paula, the Staff Nurse, told her.

'Looks like your wish will be granted. We're needed,' Lauren told him, leaving the ward quickly and setting off down the corridor to A&E.

'What have we got?' asked Tom, instantly professional.

'Three-year-old child fallen into a pond. Hit his head on some decking at the edge and stopped breathing. The ambulance crew revived him but the water was very polluted and they're concerned about residual damage.'

'Three-year-olds and water aren't a very good mix, are they?' he remarked.

'Happens all the time. Now, we should get ourselves organised.' She put on a disposable apron and gloves and went to the door as the ambulance drew up.

'Hi, Lauren,' called Jeff the paramedic, opening the back doors. 'This is David. Decided to become a duck but couldn't quite manage to float like the ducks do. He's still feeling pretty sick, aren't you, little chap?'

The child moaned and continued to wail as they lifted him out of the ambulance. His mother, hardly more than a child herself, Lauren thought, followed, looking every bit as white-faced as he did.

Lauren put out a hand to comfort her. 'We'll soon get him sorted. Try not to worry too much.'

The girl looked gratefully at her. 'I feel so bad — I only took my eyes off him for a minute. That stupid pond's going to be filled in, I don't care what his dad says. I'm not risking it again — lethal it is.'

Lauren smiled as she listened to Jeff's report, deciding in her mind what was needed next while Tom took charge. He examined the child's head to check for concussion and gently talked to the boy as he did so.

'Does your head hurt, David? Tell me if anywhere else hurts.'

Quickly and competently he assessed the child and listened to his chest.

'I don't think there's any lasting damage but he'll probably feel a bit sore for a couple of days. I'd like to keep him in for a while, for observation. We'll also give him some antibiotics, just to make sure. He may have swallowed some water. Is he allergic to anything?'

The mother shook her head, almost too scared to speak.

'Don't worry. We'll soon have him back with you, as good as new,' Tom told her.

He turned to Lauren. 'We need a bed for him. Who organises the beds?

'I'll get Paula to do it. She's our staff nurse — I'll introduce you in a minute.'

* * *

The rest of the day seemed to fly by. They dealt with the usual round of patients, some of whom could well have been treated by their own GP, but everyone seemed to prefer the small hospital, where they could turn up without an appointment.

Lauren had enjoyed working with Tom and already had a good impression of his clinical skills. There had been no time to talk about his private life, so when he asked if there was somewhere they could go for a quick drink after work, she gladly accepted.

In the locker room she changed from her hospital scrubs and swiftly pulled the pins from her hair. She shook her head, glad to be free of the restraining clips, and her dark curls tumbled to her shoulders. She brushed out a few tangles, then sprayed on a little light perfume. Glancing in the mirror, she frowned at her reflection. If she'd only thought, she would have put on something slightly more presentable than her jeans that morning. Her ten-minute walk to work never merited anything special and this morning it

13

had been raining slightly.

Ah, well, why worry? It was only a drink. She left the room and went to look for Tom.

A small knot of people were gathered in the foyer.

'Here she is at last,' Paula called out. 'Come on, Lauren! We're all dying of thirst.'

Lauren hurried forward, slightly disappointed to discover that Tom had invited everyone for a drink, not just her. Then she grinned, wondering why she was suddenly behaving like a silly, jealous teenager.

It was a jolly group and everyone agreed that Tom was going to fit in very well. The fact that most of the department were female and he was an extremely good-looking man may have had something to do with it! Despite the fact that most of them were married or engaged, they all paid him a good deal of attention.

He was very good at fending off questions, however, and all they learned

14

was that he had lived in New Zealand for the past twelve years and was ready for a change.

'I can't believe you could give up New Zealand and come to live in an isolated place like Landris,' Jenny remarked.

'Everywhere has its attractions,' he replied easily, glancing at Lauren as he spoke — something which Jenny's sharp eyes didn't miss.

'Well, I suppose I should be going,' Tom said a moment later. 'Can I drop anyone off anywhere?'

They all shook their heads and only Lauren stood up to go at the same time.

'I take it you'd like a lift? Where do you live?' he asked as they left.

'No, thanks — it's just a short walk from here, but I was ready to leave anyway,' Lauren replied. 'I'm staying in a hospital flat at the moment, but I'm looking for somewhere to buy.'

'I'm hoping to find somewhere too,' he returned. 'I'm in a small rented place myself. It's not at all suitable really, but it'll do for now.' He paused, staring at her. 'You know, I hardly recognised you with your hair loose. You should wear it that way more often. You have lovely hair.'

Her heart began beating out of control and a flush crept up her cheeks.

'It's quite impractical for a busy doctor,' she said a little breathlessly. 'I keep thinking I should get it all chopped off.'

'Don't you dare. It would be such a waste.' He reached out and touched it gently. 'Sorry but I've been wanting to do that all day — really unprofessional.'

Impulsively she reached up and ran her fingers through his hair in return.

'Well, it's only fair,' she said and they both laughed.

'Feel free. It's nice, very nice indeed. I think I'm going to enjoy my stay here very much.'

He stopped laughing and leaned closer to her. For a dizzying moment, she had the feeling he was about to kiss her . . . but he drew back abruptly.

'I'd — I'd better go. I'll see you tomorrow, Lauren.'

He fiddled with his car keys then quickly climbed into his car and shut the door. Then with a casual wave, he drove off.

She stared after him.

'Well, well, Tom Asprey. What was all that about?'

She walked back to her flat, confused and irrationally disturbed by the incident. Had she done or said something to frighten him off?

★   ★   ★

The impersonal block of flats echoed as Lauren opened the street door. She picked up several envelopes from her mail box. Two estate agents had sent details of properties and there were a couple of bills and a postcard from her mother. Italy, she noticed. Lucky Mum.

She didn't begrudge her mother's new-found happiness and was pleased

17

that her new husband had the time and money to travel with her. All the same, she wished *she* could afford the time and expense of a good holiday somewhere warm and exotic.

A wealthy, handsome man wouldn't come amiss either, she laughed to herself as she clattered up the stairs.

Listening to the babble of noise that came from the rows of identical doors, she renewed her vow to find somewhere else to live as soon as possible. She'd been saving hard ever since she'd started work and had a deposit ready to put down once she found the right place. Maybe there would be something suitable in one of today's envelopes? She hoped so.

Once inside, she poured herself a glass of fruit juice and sat down to look at what the estate agent had sent her.

To her delight, one of them looked perfect. It was a three-bedroomed cottage in the next village along the coast. It was quite expensive, but just about within her budget. Sitting-room, kitchen-diner and a small garden at the back. Perfect. She glanced at her watch. It was too late to call now but first thing in the morning she would make an appointment to view.

The phone rang just then.

'Lauren? Angus here. I just wondered how you'd got on with Dr Asprey. Is he going to fit in, do you think?'

'Angus, it's lovely to hear from you. Yes, Dr Asprey was fine. I think he'll be OK. How's it going with you? Are you getting used to being a free man again?'

They chatted easily for a few minutes. It was typical of Angus to phone to check that everything was OK, though what he would have done if she'd said no, she didn't know. Lauren smiled. Knowing Angus, he would probably have abandoned his trip.

'You go off and have a great time,' she told him. 'And don't worry — everything will be fine in Dr Tom's capable hands. Besides, he's always got me to order him about. Angus, I'm really going to miss you, you know,' she

19

said, serious for a moment. 'What shall I do without your help and advice?'

'You'll cope. Just as you always do. And you'll have Tom right there to ask, anyhow. Goodbye then, love. I'm off in the morning. America, here I come — see you in a few months.' Angus paused. 'And, Lauren — you should try to get out a bit more. You're too dedicated by half — and he's a nice man.'

Lauren laughed, but after she had put the phone down she thought about Angus's parting words.

Yes, indeed, Tom Asprey was a nice man. More than that, he was provoking thoughts in her that she had been avoiding for the past five years!

Pull yourself together, she ordered. You've only just met him and you know nothing at all about him.

Yet there was something about him. She felt drawn to him in a way she hadn't experienced in years . . . or perhaps hadn't allowed herself to experience, would be more accurate.

A Clifftop Drama

Lauren took a little more care with her clothes the next morning and even put on a light touch of make-up, something she rarely did for work.

The sun was shining as she set out for the short walk to the hospital. She was looking forward to the day. She enjoyed her work and the challenges she often faced. The joy of seeing a sick person get better and knowing she had contributed was most satisfying. There was often sadness too, of course, but like all medical workers she had to learn how to deal with each situation as it arose.

'Good morning,' Tom said as he pushed open the door for her.

'Lovely day,' she greeted him.

They walked together into the department and went to the office for the morning takeover from the night shift. It had been a quiet night with nothing left outstanding for them to follow up.

'I think we've time for a quick coffee then,' Tom suggested. 'How do you take it?'

'Black, no sugar, please,' Lauren replied, surprised that he was getting it for her.

She glanced at her watch. It was too early to ring the estate agent, but she must do it as soon as possible.

'So, tell me about yourself,' Tom invited as they sat back to enjoy their coffee.

'There's not a lot to tell.' She gave him brief details of her career so far, and said nothing at all about her private life.

'And what do you enjoy doing when you're not at work?' he asked.

'Walking, swimming. I don't know really. I'm always exhausted after work and tend to slump in front of the television or play music. Sometimes a crowd of us go out for a meal or to the pub. What about you?'

'I haven't really had much time for hobbies. I have to . . . ' He broke off as a bell rang. Lauren picked up the phone.

'Yes? OK. We're ready for you.' She hung up. 'RTA coming in. Two injured but they think it's minor. Car and motorbike ran into each other.'

They leapt into action, selecting the protective clothing and pulling on gloves.

As the trolleys were wheeled in, the usual run-down of suspected injuries and observations were related by the ambulance teams and both doctors concentrated on their two patients.

As suggested, there was little wrong with them apart from minor abrasions and shock, and once they'd been examined and assessed, the nurses stepped in to clean them up and apply stitches and dressings.

'I'll go and start the ward rounds,' Tom suggested. 'Page me if you need me. I want to take a look at little David

— make sure there have been no repercussions.'

'Fine. I'll get on with some paperwork, until the next interruption.'

She settled down at the desk with a sigh, preparing to deal with the heap of forms. This was probably everyone's least favourite task, she thought.

Before she started, however, she remembered the property she wanted to look at and phoned the estate agent, making an appointment for the following evening. The cheerful agent told her that there was already a great deal of interest in the cottage.

Blow, she thought as she hung up. If other people were looking around, it meant the sellers were unlikely to accept an offer. She'd been hoping they might, so that she'd have a little left over to spend on furnishings and all the other paraphernalia that would be needed.

Ah well, she could always scrounge a few bits and pieces until she could afford to furnish the place the way she wanted.

She pulled herself back to reality with an effort — she hadn't even seen the place yet and here she was practically working out colour schemes!

She drew the pile of forms closer and began to write.

A short while later, the peace outside was broken by a loud wailing, together with a parent's voice obviously scolding her child.

'I don't care what you wanted to do. You go climbing on rocks when I distinctly tell you not to, you have to come here and have it seen to. Understand?'

The wailing ceased and deep sobs could be heard.

Lauren went out to survey the damage.

'Hello,' she said with a smile. 'What have you been up to?'

The child looked at her mother, not daring to say anything.

'Stupid little thing fell off the rocks. I told her not to go there. Didn't I tell you not to go?' the mother said, giving the child a shake. 'Now look what's happened.' She turned to Lauren. 'You take 'em to the beach and this is what they do to you.' She glared at the child again. 'You'll have to have stitches and you know how much needles hurt.'

The child began to wail again.

'Why don't you go and get yourself a coffee?' Lauren suggested to the irate woman. 'You need it for the shock. We'll soon patch up your little girl. What's her name?'

'Kylie. I could certainly do with a cuppa. Been on the go all day I have. You sure you don't mind?'

'Not at all. We'll be fine, won't we, Kylie?' Lauren smiled at the child, who nodded, looking relieved.

'Didn't want Mum to shout — but it 'urts,' she whispered, as her mother left and Lauren led her into a treatment room.

'I know. Don't worry, we'll soon have you fixed up. I've got some special tape here. We can use that instead of stitches and you'll hardly notice.'

'Me mum 'ates needles. So I do as well.'

Lauren smiled. It was so easy for parents to transfer their own fears on to their children.

'OK. I'm afraid this might sting a bit,' she said. 'But I need to clean up the cut to make sure there's nothing nasty in there.'

She worked quickly, applying butterfly tapes to the long, shallow slash, chatting to the child all the while to reassure her. With any luck, her calm attitude would prevent her being frightened of hospitals again.

Any of the nursing staff could have done this task but Lauren wanted to be doing something . . . anything rather than paperwork!

By the time her mother returned, little Kylie was sitting happily chatting, a large dressing stuck over her little leg.

A couple more minor injuries were sorted out and treated, and then Lauren was back in the office. She was bored with the tedious chore and wondered why Tom had been away for so long.

As if drawn by her thoughts, he came into the little office and Lauren noticed her heart gave a leap at the sight of him.

'Hi, there,' she said as casually as her voice would allow. 'Seen everything you needed to?'

'Fine. It's a good place. I like the convenient size of it all. I can speak to every patient if I want to, without a ten-mile hike to get there. Makes a change after the huge places where you never get to know anyone — patients or staff. But it must be lunch-time now — are you coming to the canteen?'

'It's hardly a canteen! But they do some good snacks. Didn't you go down there yesterday?'

'I brought my own sandwiches yesterday but I didn't have time to make them this morning. I had too much to do. Come on then — I'll buy you a sandwich.'

He held out a hand to pull her out of her chair. Embarrassed, she took it and felt his strong grip around her own small hand. He looked at her with such an intense gaze that she felt compelled to look away.

'What is it?' she said at last. 'Have I got something on my chin?'

'I was trying to decide whether your eyes are blue or green.'

'And did you decide?'

'Blue. Definitely blue. With a greenish tinge. Or green with a blueish tinge.'

'What kind of sandwiches do you like?' She blurted out the question to cover the confusion she was feeling and only succeeded in making herself feel silly. What had that to do with the colour of her eyes? Why did she feel tongue-tied whenever they were together? It was easy when they were dealing with patients, but otherwise . . .

She watched him as he spoke to the other staff. Even Maggie in the canteen was treated to a dose of his charm. He obviously enjoyed meeting other people and by the way he touched everyone, casual gestures, it became more and more obvious that he was one of nature's more physical beings.

Gradually Lauren was coming to realise that it was entirely his nature and that he held everyone's hand for slightly longer than necessary and touched people on the arm more than most, giving the impression of a feeling of intimacy.

She pressed her lips together. She'd been reading something into his behaviour towards her that simply wasn't there. She took a deep breath and vowed that she must stop thinking of Dr Tom Asprey as anything more than a pleasant colleague. She'd fallen for a charmer once before and it had nearly ruined her life.

★　★　★

They were just finishing their lunch when both their pagers sounded at the same time. Exchanging a quick glance, they both rose and almost ran back to A&E, where they found Paula looking anxious.

'We've got an emergency — a man's fallen down the cliff, off Landris Head. The rescue helicopter's at the scene but there's apparently an overhang and they can't get in close enough. He's taken a bad fall and seems to be wedged in a cleft in the rocks. He probably needs treatment on site. Looks like a bad one. There's an ambulance on the way, but they want a doctor there.'

'I'll go,' Tom said immediately. 'I've done plenty of climbing in my time. Do we have an emergency kit ready?'

'Of course. But you might have to walk a bit. There's no vehicle access to the spot.'

'How do I find it? Is there a map or guidance system?'

'I'll come too,' Lauren offered. 'I can show you. You may need help.'

'But we can't leave the department without a doctor . . .'

'There are at least two other doctors in the hospital today,' Paula cut in. 'The dermatology consultant's doing his minor ops clinic and Dr Mac's doing his outpatients. We're covered if there's another emergency. Go on. Both of you, go.'

'Right. Grab a jacket and go and get your car. It'll be easier than waiting for the response vehicle,' Lauren said. 'I'll bring the bags.'

Tom didn't argue and grabbed the luminous green and yellow jacket with *Doctor* flashed across the back. He ran out to the car park and drove his car round to the front entrance, leaving his hazard lights flashing as he jumped out to help Lauren with the heavy bags of emergency medical gear.

'All set?' he asked as they fastened their seat belts.

She nodded and gave him directions to the Head. There was a car park but it was some distance from the accident site, or where she understood it to be. They stopped near a gate where someone was waiting.

'Doctors,' Tom called to him.

'You can get through here,' the man replied, 'and if you're careful you can get a bit closer.'

They bumped over the rough ground until the sea and the cliff edge were in sight. They stopped and grabbed their jackets and the medical kits, half running to the spot where a few people were gathered. An almost hysterical woman was being comforted by someone dressed in hiking gear. An air ambulance was hovering overhead and he began to descend, looking for a safe place to put down.

'Can someone fill us in?' Tom asked.

'It's my husband,' the woman wailed. 'The dog fell down the cliff and he tried to reach it. Then he slipped himself and now he's stuck. Oh please, do something. He mustn't die. You can't let him die.'

'We'll do all we can. Has anyone got a hot drink for her?'

One of the crowd of watchers came forward with a flask and poured something hot. Several of them clustered round the victim's wife, offering words of comfort. Satisfied that everything was under control there, Lauren went to the edge of the cliff to Tom. He was lying on the ground, peering over. She joined him.

'I can only just see him,' he said. 'Looks as if he's wedged in a cleft in the rock. He isn't moving at all so he's either unconscious or . . . '

'How on earth are we going to get down there?'

'We aren't. Not at this stage. I need ropes and pegs. I'd be better with climbing boots but I'll have to manage.'

'The helicopter's landed. They'll have all the gear for this sort of thing. They're on their way now.' Lauren stood up and beckoned to the air ambulance crew.

As the two men in red ran across the field towards them, Tom leapt up and ran to meet them. He issued rapid instructions and the two returned to the helicopter to collect equipment, including safety helmets and red overalls for the two doctors.

Tom was looking down the cliff again, working out a route he could take. He looked around for a large rock to anchor the ropes and then a way to reach the stranded climber. It was a tricky call. The man was some distance to one side of where the ropes could go down. Tom would have to climb around the overhang to reach him, and then came the problem of how to get them all back up.

'How can we reach him?' Lauren asked.

'Like I said, there's no *we*. I'm going down with one of the crew. Presumably they have experience in this sort of rescue. I want you up here. You can send down anything extra we need.'

Lauren's heart was pounding. She felt a huge sense of relief that Tom didn't want her to climb down. She was terrified of heights. If it hadn't been for a time spent rock-climbing in her student days, her life would have taken a very different turn. She would never have been in this situation now. If she'd been needed, however, she would have had no choice but to grit her teeth and make the hazardous trip down the cliff.

'You want us to go down first and assess the situation?' one of the air crew asked. 'I'm Alan — this is Joe.'

'One of you can come down with me. I think I'm certainly needed down there — he's not moving at all. What equipment have you got?'

'We've got all you'll need,' said Joe.

Alan was peering down the cliff and making the same assessment that Tom had made: 'Not an easy spot. We'll have to traverse across, see the exact situation and then work out how to get him up.'

Quickly the ropes were sorted, helmets issued and the two men buckled their harnesses. Joe secured the ropes at the top and watched, carefully feeding out the line as Alan climbed down first.

Once Alan had secured the ropes to a peg hammered into a cleft in the rocks, he waved to Tom.

Tom attached himself to the ropes and began the long climb down.

'He knows what he's doing,' Joe reassured Lauren as her scared eyes followed him down. 'Alan's making the traverse now . . . ' he reported.

Lauren lay down on the ground again, watching breathlessly as the two men slowly climbed towards the injured man.

At their signal, Joe lowered the cliff rescue stretcher, laden with the equipment they were likely to need, then switched on his two-way radio.

Tom's voice crackled back: 'He's still alive but he's unconscious. We think he may have injured his back — and one foot's jammed into the rocks and twisted round. It's all looking pretty nasty.'

'The sledge is near you. Alan knows what's what,' said Joe.

Lauren watched as they pulled the stretcher — or sledge as Joe called it — towards them. She saw them give the trapped man some oxygen, and sent up her own prayers for a successful outcome.

She heard someone approaching and turned to look.

'He's dead, isn't he?' the man's wife whimpered. 'My Jack's dead.'

'No, he isn't,' Lauren assured her. 'The doctor's with him now. Don't worry, those are two very experienced men down there — they'll take care of him. Now, come on, let's find you somewhere to wait — we need to leave the experts to do their job.'

The woman was shaking with fear and more likely to get in the way than be able to help. Besides, it meant they didn't have to guard their words if she was out of the way.

The group of bystanders was growing. Lauren wondered where they had all come from but it was always the same — see a helicopter landing and people appeared from all over.

'Need any help, love?' a large man driving a four-by-four asked. 'This thing'll go anywhere.'

Lauren was aware that he had driven quite illegally over the farmland, but she might as well make use of his offer of help.

'You could let this lady sit in the warm, if you don't mind. It's her husband who's fallen. We'll let you know as soon as there's any news.'

Lauren went back to the edge of the cliff to see what was needed. Despite her inner fear and dread, she knew that she would do whatever was necessary to save this man's life.

'They're having problems,' Joe announced when she returned to the cliff top. 'He's in and out of consciousness. They've given him morphine for the pain. Seems they can't un-jam his foot without moving him, and they can't get him on to the spinal board while he's still trapped by the foot.'

'They surely won't need to amputate, will they? The shock could be too much for him stuck out there.' She bit her lip. 'Suppose I went down as well? Alan might be able to pull his foot out while Tom and I hold him?'

'I could go down but I'm really

needed here to co-ordinate. Have you been down before?' Joe asked.

In a small, slightly quaking voice, she assured him that she had. She didn't add that if she hadn't been climbing before, she might have been the mother of a child of . . . what would it have been? Five years old?

'Hang on — I'll ask them what they need.'

He spoke into the radio: 'Alan? Lauren here's offered to come down to help.'

'We could certainly use another pair of hands, but it's a bit hairy,' Alan's muffled voice came back.

'If she's sure. Tell her to be careful,' Tom's voice interrupted.

Lauren grabbed a harness and buckled it in place. She was already wearing a safety helmet and she attached herself to the rope as Joe fed it out.

'OK — climbing.'

★ ★ ★

40

She set her trembling feet down to the first ledge. The need for her help quelled her fears and she simply got on with what she had to do. She abseiled a short way down and then climbed steadily to the ledge, where she detached the climbing rope and clipped herself to the rope they'd set up for the traverse. Adrenaline kicked in and she forgot her fears.

Soon she reached the two men and listened carefully as Tom explained the problem.

'We can slide a short board behind his back to steady things. Then I think if Alan gently twists his leg and we support his torso, once the foot's released, we can slide the spinal board under him.'

'Looking at the angle, there's a danger it could break his leg,' she remarked.

'It could, but it's a better risk than amputation. The shock of that could kill him.'

'Shall I untie his boot? That might

help.' She reached awkwardly across the inert body and tried to untie his laces. When that didn't work, she reached into her pocket and took out her scissors and snipped the laces. 'I reckon the foot might slip out better now.'

'Right. Let's do it,' Alan ordered crisply. 'Everyone got him? Go.'

The two doctors held the man's torso firmly, minimising any movement, while Alan grasped the leg. With a final sickening wrench, the foot slipped out of the boot and the imprisoning rock. They wouldn't know if anything was broken until he was X-rayed at the hospital.

Quickly they strapped their patient to the stretcher and secured his head between the foam blocks. He briefly regained consciousness and mumbled something incoherent.

'Don't worry — you're on your way to hospital. Keep as still as you can,' Tom said to him.

The only response was a moan.

'We'll need to get some fluids into

him as soon as we're up top,' Tom said.

Lauren was impressed by his cool assessment of the situation and his practical handling of everything.

He smiled across at her and she felt her heart turn over at the compassion and understanding in his eyes. However, then she saw his mouth compress into a hard line as he glanced along the cliff ledge.

'Well done. That was the easy bit. Now we have to get him along to clear the overhang.'

'If we can get him to that flat bit of rock, the chopper can probably lift him from there,' Alan suggested.

The three of them manoeuvred themselves to a position where they could slide the stretcher along, inches at a time. Alan went first with Tom supporting the other end, while Lauren carefully freed the ropes from the treacherous rocks which tried their best to snatch at them, snagging them and making movement impossible.

'Stop here,' Alan ordered once they

reached their goal.

He pulled out his radio and spoke to Joe, telling him of the plan. Between them they decided Lauren should climb back to the top and stay by the ropes securing them to the rocks while Joe fetched the chopper and lowered the cable to pick them up. They could then be winched into the helicopter and flown to Truro, the nearest major hospital.

The adrenaline was flowing in the doctors and rescue crew and they seemed to be accomplishing tasks which normally they might all have considered beyond them.

'You OK with that, Lauren? Can you manage to climb back up the cliff on your own and take over from Joe?'

'Of course,' she said, trying not to think about it too much. Sliding down was relatively easy but the long haul back was another matter.

'Good girl,' Tom said, grasping her arm briefly. 'Take care and don't hurry yourself. You're a very precious part of our team.'

She smiled at his encouraging words and began the climb.

She felt an upward tug on the rope and glanced up to Joe, high above her. He was pulling the ropes as she climbed, taking some of the weight from her aching limbs. It was a wonderful help and she reached the top far sooner than she'd expected.

Quickly she undid the harness and took the radio from Joe. While he ran back towards the helicopter, she radioed down to the men waiting below.

'Safely up. Won't be long. Joe's almost back at the chopper now. Everything OK with you?'

'Holding on,' Tom's voice came back.

The roar of the helicopter drowned further comment and soon it was hovering above them all. Slowly Joe lowered the winch . . .

It deflected in the wind but was soon low enough to allow it to swing towards the waiting men. Alan caught it and attached the huge hook to the stretcher, stepping on to the loops of webbing and securing them with long-practised ease. It allowed him to rise with the injured man, guiding the sledge as it neared the open door. Painfully slowly, it seemed to those watching, they were winched into the helicopter before they at last flew away from the cliff.

Tom was already beginning the climb back, his movements economical and easy, obviously those of an experienced climber.

As the helicopter touched down on the grass once more, the injured man's wife came running across the grass, stooping low for fear of the blades.

'Is he all right?' she called.

'He'll be fine . . .'

The crew helped her into the helicopter and seconds later they were airborne again, heading for the hospital at Truro.

Lauren helped Tom up the last few feet and they both sank on the ground, exhausted. Lauren was aware of a great sense of anti-climax.

'You were fantastic, Tom.'

'You were pretty good yourself — came just at the right time. Have you done much climbing?'

'Not since uni. I . . . I gave it up,' she said briefly. 'I had a fall. But that was a long time ago now.'

'You climbed down there when you were terrified?' Tom said incredulously. 'Now that really *is* brave.'

He reached out to take her hand but suddenly reaction set in and she was shaking and tearful.

'Hey, hey, it's all right.' He put his arms round her and held her close, stroking her hair gently. She felt wonderfully warm and safe. 'Come on now. It's all over. They'll take good care of him in Truro.'

'They've left all their gear here. I've still got the radio and the harness and everything,' she sobbed.

'I'm sure one of these guys will take it all back.'

Lauren looked up. A huge crowd had gathered round them, with the police, coastguards and an ambulance all a little distance away. Someone pushed their way through the crowd and before they knew it a microphone was thrust in their faces.

'Radio Cornwall. Can you tell us what happened here? Is the man all right?'

They both stood up, Tom with his arm round Lauren's shoulders to support her. He spoke clearly, outlining the events, and adding that a bulletin would probably be issued from the hospital later when the full extent of the man's injuries was known.

'Would you like to comment on the dangers of holiday-makers walking near the cliffs? It seems to be a common problem during the holiday season. Do you know why he was so close to the edge?'

'Oh, heavens, there was a dog!' Lauren remembered. 'His dog fell over and he was trying to reach it.'

'I doubt any dog could have survived that fall,' Tom said. 'I'm sorry but there's nothing we can do. It's too risky

48

to go down again.'

'Maybe the lifeboat will find him,' the reporter suggested.

Lauren looked down and saw the small orange inshore lifeboat bobbing near the rocks far below. If by some miracle the dog had fallen into the sea, they might be able to find it. But the chances were very slim.

As a ripple of applause from the crowd and cries of 'Well done' reached her, Lauren smiled wanly and Tom raised his hand in acknowledgment.

The police and ambulance crew were collecting the equipment to return to the air ambulance. They were free to leave.

The Perfect House

'Come on, Lauren. We'd better get back. You need some hot, sweet tea.' Tom's warm hand took hers and they went back to the car, parked what seemed a lifetime ago near a field gate.

'I think a large brandy might be better,' she moaned.

'That had better be later. Much later. Maybe we could go out for a drink later on?'

Two days running, Lauren thought. People will talk, but who cares?

'Thanks. I'd love to,' she said.

The drive back to the hospital held an almost dreamlike quality after the drama. Lauren felt unbelievably weary. Tom smiled at her and reached for her hand, giving it a reassuring squeeze. She tried to make herself believe it was just his way and that he would make contact with anyone in this way. But somehow, the thought didn't ring true. She felt a bond growing between them — a bond based on something so strongly physical that it made her catch her breath.

He, on the other hand, sounded quite calm as he spoke.

'Well, here we are. Let's see what's been happening in our absence.'

They went inside and hung up their fluorescent emergency jackets.

Lauren went into the cloakroom to freshen up a little. She was still rather shaken and though she hoped she had put on a good performance for Tom on the way back, she still felt a little weepy. At the same time though, she was extremely proud of herself for having conquered her fear of heights.

She went into the reception area where everyone was grouped round Tom, listening to his account of the day.

'Here she comes — quite the heroine,' Jenny called out.

'No, I'm not. It was all down to Tom. He was brilliant.' Lauren took the cup of hot tea she was offered, tasted it and pulled a face. 'Ugh! I hate tea at the best of times but this must have half a pound of sugar in it!'

'Doctor's orders. I don't know what you've been up to but he was most insistent that your blood sugar should be replenished,' Jenny teased.

'A bar of chocolate would have been better. So what's been going on here?'

'We've had a very quiet afternoon — a few minors, nothing we couldn't handle. You might as well go home. I expect you need a rest after all your adventures. We can do the hand-over.' Paula smiled at her and Lauren nodded gratefully.

'Thanks. I could do with a change of clothes and a shower. If you're sure? Thanks, I owe you one. If you're sure you don't mind, Tom?'

'No problem. I won't be far behind you. Once I do the hand-over, I'll make for home myself.'

As she went to the locker-room, to her surprise he followed her in.

'About that drink,' he began, 'why don't we make it supper? I could pick you up around seven?'

'That sounds good. Thank you.'

He looked pleased. 'Give me your address and think of somewhere nice to go. I don't know anywhere around here. Apart from the local corner shop, I've seen nothing.'

Lauren jotted down her address.

'Better let me have your phone number as well, in case anything crops up,' he suggested.

* * *

Lauren flopped on to her bed when she got home. She was utterly worn out, but the tumult of feelings racing through her mind and body kept her awake. Tom Asprey had awoken an awareness in her that she had been stifling for several years. She hadn't been without offers but somehow she had never dared to allow herself to get close to anyone.

53

Adam had hurt her far too much for that.

His handsome face slipped into her mind. He'd been so good looking, she'd hardly been able to believe he could be interested in her, a mere third-year student, the year below him. But he had and they'd gone out together for a year — a frantic, exciting year. She had really believed it was going to be for ever, and when he'd asked her to marry him, she'd said yes.

It had all seemed so exciting and right at the time when they'd married secretly, not even telling her parents — they would never have understood. But she had been young and in love and all too trusting.

When she'd accidentally become pregnant, she'd been thrilled but apprehensive about telling Adam. The timing had been far from perfect. She'd not seen him as a father, somehow — and, as it turned out, neither had he.

She had still been shocked, though,

when he'd refused to discuss the situation at all.

She felt tears burning her eyes even now, after all these years. She'd loved Adam so much and had foolishly believed he loved her — that they would be together for ever. Despite her condition, she'd gone with him on the university climbing club weekend as planned, desperately hoping that it would give her the chance to persuade him that their baby was a source of joy.

'But you got your way in the end, didn't you, Adam?' she whispered.

The pain was still here, despite the passing of the years. She could still cry over the terrible loss she had suffered.

Adam had remained stubbornly silent on the matter until that final dreadful day. She had continued to climb with the group, not wanting any of the others to guess her condition. But perhaps it was her condition that had made her lose concentration . . .

When she'd slipped and fallen, she had crashed against the rock face. She would never forget that feeling as she'd swung helplessly, hanging from the safety harness which had saved her life but not that of her baby. The miscarriage had come a couple of hours later.

It had been still early in the pregnancy and her recovery had scarcely interrupted her studies.

As for Adam, he had been sympathetic but obviously relieved that the problem had been so neatly solved. Only a matter of weeks later, he'd gone off on another climbing trip with friends, leaving her knowing that she'd made the worst mistake of her life in marrying him.

But worse was yet to come. Her world had seemed to end when the news came that Adam had been killed. Always a foolhardy, dare-devil climber, this time he'd taken things too far, with calamitous results.

She had been devastated, but in a strange way she had felt as if she had escaped further heartache later on.

'You were never exactly the caring type, were you, Adam?' she muttered.

All these years later, she could still feel the acute pain of the loss of her baby and her first love. However, perhaps at last she was ready to move on and start again. Tom was certainly making her think of things she'd been pushing aside for much too long. She was only twenty-eight, for heaven's sake. She surely wasn't intending to remain single for all of her life? All the same, allowing a man — any man and especially a charming man like Tom Asprey — into her closely-guarded heart was something to be considered with great care.

Thoughtfully she showered and changed. She brushed her hair and left it loose. Hadn't Tom said he liked it that way? Not that she wanted to please him especially . . .

He was late. Almost quarter of an hour. She tried not to let it matter. It was only a casual evening, after all.

The phone rang and it was him,

apologising, saying it would be a few more minutes before he left home.

'Thanks for letting me know,' she said calmly.

She wandered round the tiny flat, tidying already tidy cushions and pushing the books level in her packed bookcase. Why was she so nervous? Perhaps it was the strain of the afternoon catching up with her.

Whatever the reason, she was pleased when at last she saw his car pulling into the close. She hurried out and ran down the stairs, partly to avoid the awkwardness of him coming up to look for her.

'Hi. I thought I'd save you the climb. You've done enough of that for one day,' she said lightly.

'My legs do feel a bit like lead. I'm so out of condition! I must find a gym and some time to use it. You look good.'

'Thank you. You don't look so bad yourself.'

She got into his large, four-wheel-drive car for the second time that day.

'Which way?' he asked.

'Down to the end of the road and turn left. There's a nice pub in the next village where they do lovely food. We can sit outside as long as the weather holds.'

★ ★ ★

It was a pleasant evening. The shared stress of the day brought them close and they felt comfortable in each other's company.

'Do you want to talk about your fear of heights? It might help.'

'Maybe, but don't let's spoil this evening. I just want to enjoy the view and this delicious chilli — I'm starving.'

'Me too. I'd like to know more about you though. Everything there is to know.' As he touched her hand and held it gently, her heart turned over. She felt herself drawn towards him more and more.

'I . . . ' she began.

'Excuse me. I don't like to interrupt

— but you're the two doctors who saved that man this afternoon, aren't you? Out on the cliffs?'

'Well, yes,' Tom admitted, turning to the woman who'd stopped by their table.

'I thought so. I said to my husband, that's those two doctors. How is the poor man?'

The woman was one of the group who'd been watching. Evidently she was the one who had supplied the hot drink and as such it had made her part of the team, in her eyes at least.

Tom quietly explained that the victim of the accident was in Treliske Hospital in Truro and that he knew nothing more at this stage. However, she didn't take the hint and hung around prattling for the next few minutes.

'Excuse me if I carry on eating — our food is getting cold,' Tom said at last.

'Oh, I'm sorry. But it was all so exciting — though I expect it's all in your day's work. Oh, I'm sorry. Sorry to interrupt.' At last she went away.

However, their previous intimate mood was impossible to recapture.

'Well, at least we gave them something to talk about for the rest of the year,' Tom said dryly and they continued to eat in silence.

'Do you want pudding?' Tom asked. 'They have some interesting sounding dishes on the board.'

'I'm in the mood to indulge in something very chocolatey,' she admitted.

'And a black coffee, no sugar, to follow?'

'Right.' She was impressed that he remembered.

It was nine-thirty when he began looking at his watch.

'Look, I'm sorry but I'm bushed. Do you mind if we call it a day?'

'Not at all. I'm pretty weary too. It's been quite a day and tomorrow starts at seven-thirty.'

He went inside to pay and she stood looking out over the sea. Distant lights twinkled and she thought of the fishermen out there, working through the night. How different people's lives were. She usually only came into contact with them at times of stress and injury.

Tom came and stood behind her, slipping his arm round her waist.

'Penny for them?'

'I was just thinking about the diversity of life. You must find it very different here. Is New Zealand as beautiful as everyone says?'

'I guess so. Some things are terrific. The medical services are good and it's easy to call in other specialities. Attitudes are changing now. They always said it was twenty years behind in many ways, but I think they're catching up and even overtaking us here, in other ways.'

'So why come back? Our NHS is always under fire.'

'It's a very long story and like I said, I've had it for today. Come on,' he said softly, taking her arm and leading her to his car.

Neither of them spoke during the short journey. He stopped outside her door. Should she invite him in?

'Would you . . . ' she began.

'Thanks, but no,' he replied. 'There's a lot you don't know about me, yet. I . . . er . . . never mind now. It's late. Believe me, I could grow to like you an awful lot, Lauren. It just isn't the right time.'

'I see. Well, thanks for the meal. My turn next time — if there is a next time.'

'I'd like that. See you tomorrow.'

She climbed out of the car and slammed the door shut. She had been half expecting him to kiss her but he had made no sign of wanting to do so. She gave him a casual wave and went inside.

It was strange, she thought. He seemed quite open one minute and was pulling away the next. He was quite an enigma.

★   ★   ★

The next day was frantically busy. She scarcely saw Tom at all as she went from patient to patient in a steady stream. Skin complaints, upset tummies and one suspected angina case filled her day. She visited her patients on the wards and wrote reports.

It was almost the end of her shift before Tom finally caught up with her.

'Look, I feel I owe you some explanation. Can we have a chat when we're through here?'

'OK,' she said slowly. 'But I don't know what you mean. Really, it doesn't matter.'

'No, I feel I want to explain things. Just for half an hour?'

'OK — oh, no, I'm sorry,' she suddenly remembered. 'I've got an appointment this evening. Maybe later on?'

'Oh, strewth — so have I. Got an appointment, I mean. I'd quite forgotten. We'd better make it some other time.' He suddenly looked extremely weary. 'What time is it? It feels like it must be about midnight.'

'It's only five-thirty,' she told him. 'In fact, I'm going to have to get a move on if I'm going to make my appointment.'

'Hot date, is it?'

She laughed. 'No such luck! How about yours?' she countered.

'Nothing like that for me either.'

She collected her briefcase and set out for home. She had half an hour before her appointment with the estate agent, so even allowing for the drive there, she would be in plenty of time.

Trying to push the events of the day to the back of her mind, she concentrated on the prospect of viewing a possible new home and began to feel quite excited.

She wondered what Tom was doing that evening and realised she was experiencing a pang of jealousy. What was it he wanted to tell her, she wondered. Well, there was nothing she could do about it at the moment, so her curiosity would just have to wait.

'Dr Fletcher?' the young estate agent approached her car when she stopped outside the cottage. He looked about fifteen and positively reeked of after shave.

'Yes.' She smiled and held out her hand. 'You must be Trevor?'

'That's right. Welcome to Abby's Cottage. Do come in. The owner's away at present so we have the place to ourselves.'

He opened the door and led her inside, and for Lauren it was love at first sight. It was perfect. The lounge had a long, low window with a sea view, and once she'd viewed the rest of the place she found it was everything she had dreamed of.

'It's exactly what I've been looking for,' she told the agent. She didn't bother going through the pretence of saying that it might be all right if only they would drop the price. 'I'll have it.'

'Oh, I see — great! But I'm afraid it's not that straightforward. The owner's away, as I said. I'll certainly put in your offer, but I should tell you there's another viewer coming this evening and another tomorrow.'

'Are you trying to tell me you want me to offer more?'

'Well, no, not exactly. But, in all fairness, the person making the best offer . . . it is in my client's interest, of course.'

'I'll offer the asking price. If that's not acceptable, I'm afraid I can't do any better.' She felt angry with frustration. 'I'm not in any chain and the money's virtually in place. Surely that's worth something?'

'Of course that'll all be taken into account . . . Is there anything else you'd like to see?' Trevor said uneasily. 'The next client is due at half-past.'

'Yes. I'd like to see the loft,' Lauren said.

'The loft?' he echoed, surprised.

'Yes. It says in the details there's a

loft ladder, so it shouldn't be a problem. Should it?'

'No, of course not. It's just that . . . '

'Your next client is due — I know. Well, he or she will have to wait, won't they?'

She had no desire at all to see the loft but for some reason she felt like being awkward. After all, she had just made a verbal offer on the place — surely she was entitled to have a good look?

Resignedly Trevor led the way upstairs and pulled down the ladder for her to go up and look at the loft.

She made various noises, as if she knew what she was looking at.

Just when she knew she could delay it no longer, she heard a knock at the door.

'Ah, I expect that will be . . . '

'Your next client,' she finished and he laughed uncomfortably up at her, framed in the loft hatch.

'Well, go and let them in. You mustn't keep a prospective buyer waiting.'

She didn't know why she was being

so difficult with the young man. Perhaps it was the disappointment of finding her perfect home and not being able to clinch the deal immediately.

'Dr Asprey,' she heard. 'Nice to meet you. I'm Trevor . . . '

Flabbergasted, she made her way slowly down the stairs.

'Hello, Tom,' she said.

She was about to joke about coincidences but the words stuck in her throat. Standing beside him was a child, a young boy of about five. There was no doubting his parentage. His eyes and brown hair were exactly like his father's. There was also a young woman with them. She looked a little young to be Tom's wife and the boy's mother but they were obviously a family.

'Lauren! What a surprise!' Tom said. 'I was . . . this is . . . I . . . '

'I have to go,' Lauren interrupted. 'So sorry. You'll call me tomorrow?' she said to the hapless Trevor as she pushed past the group.

Outside, she went swiftly to her car without a backward glance. She wanted to scream but she didn't know if it was with anger, with frustration or simply at her own stupidity.

A Very Trying Day

'How could he?' she kept asking herself. 'Whatever did he tell his wife when he took me out to dinner?'

After several minutes of stamping around her flat, giving her defenceless cushions the odd kick of frustration, Lauren pulled herself together and peered into the fridge to see what she could have for supper. It was then that she remembered she hadn't been shopping.

Her disappointed eye fell on a drop of wine left in a bottle. She poured it into a mug and swallowed it quickly. It tasted distinctly nasty.

'Calm down, Lauren,' she instructed herself. 'Nothing happened. You simply allowed yourself to dream a little. To lower your guard.'

Forcing herself to breathe more slowly, she sat down and switched on the television. A medical drama was just beginning. She tried to watch it for a few minutes but found herself automatically correcting procedures and turned it off in irritation.

Her mind was still whirling around the recent events. Her pleasure in finding the cottage and making an offer was totally marred by the meeting with Tom and his family. His wife looked very young — almost too young to have a child of that age. What was he? About five? Six years old? Just a bit older than her own lost baby might have been . . . She sighed. Tom's child looked just like him. Quite gorgeous, she thought, a new knot of emotion creeping into her chest and making her feel deeply sad.

'Who would believe it — after all this time, I find someone special and then discover he's married,' she whispered to the battered teddy sitting on her windowsill.

Her stomach rumbled and she went to search the cupboards. There must surely be something she could heat up for supper?

One tin of soup and some slightly stale crackers didn't make much of a meal but it was the best she could do and it was almost nutritious, she tried to convince herself.

She forced herself to think about the cottage, just to take her mind off Tom. It was simply perfect, everything she could have wanted, but would it ever be hers? There was Tom's family after it for one thing, not to mention the other people Trevor had mentioned.

Despite these negative feelings, she allowed herself to fantasise for a few moments, picturing the little garden filled with flowers and a few herbs growing in tubs by the kitchen door. She could make one of the bedrooms into an office, and once she'd established herself she'd be able to get herself on the internet and do some research projects.

After a while, sick of mooning around, she changed into her running shorts and a vest top and went out for a jog. Though it was almost dark, she knew it was the best way to clear her mind, or she would never sleep. Whatever her heart was telling her, she knew that from now on, she must avoid being alone with Tom as much as possible. Her own feelings were just too intense — especially knowing that he was also attracted to her. He was definitely forbidden fruit now.

Thank heaven they had both stepped back in time. How much worse would it have been if she'd actually followed her instincts and encouraged him to come back to the flat with her? When was that? Only two nights ago? No wonder he'd stopped so abruptly. It had rankled at the time. Pity he hadn't had the decency to tell her exactly why at that point, she thought bitterly. It might have saved a lot of upset.

By the time she arrived back at her flat, she was breathless and hot. After a quick shower, she changed into her nightshirt. It was after all that that she glanced at the answering machine and saw the light was flashing.

She played the message.

'Lauren? If you're there, please pick up.' Tom's slight New Zealand accent seemed more noticeable on the phone. 'OK. Either you don't want to answer or you're not at home. I want to explain. It isn't what it seems. Maybe I'll catch up with you at the hospital tomorrow. I really need to explain . . . er . . . 'bye then.'

It was too late to call back now, and in any case, she couldn't trust herself to speak to him. It would be far better to speak to him casually at work and try to re-establish a cool, calm working relationship with him.

★   ★   ★

Fortunately the next morning was frantically busy. The waiting-room filled up very early and both doctors were kept occupied with a mixture of minor injuries and one or two more serious matters.

Lauren managed to avoid being alone with Tom and only called for his opinion once.

An elderly farmer had come in bleeding profusely from a cut hand. As she dealt with his injury, she noticed that he was exhibiting signs that could indicate a developing heart condition. Tom agreed with her and the man was sent for further tests, X-rays and a thorough examination by the specialist, Dr Mac as he was affectionately known.

At her first opportunity, she went to the snack bar for some sandwiches. She was starving after her meagre supper the night before, and getting in early had meant she'd missed breakfast. It also meant that she could avoid any confrontation with Tom.

'What's up with you today?' asked Jenny. 'You seem a bit under the weather — distinctly grumpy. Are you sickening for something?'

'I didn't sleep too well,' Lauren muttered.

'How was the cottage? You did go to see it, didn't you?'

'Yes, and it was gorgeous. Just what I'm looking for. But there are others after it.' Lauren sighed. 'I offered the asking price but I think the agent's set on more.'

'Maybe the others will drop out — or find the price too high and offer less,' Jenny said, trying to be encouraging.

'I don't think so. Our new and esteemed leader was among the other interested parties, as it happens.'

'You mean Tom? Well, well. Looks as if he plans to stay here for a while then. You want to get in there right away. Maybe you could share the place — it'd save a lot of money,' Jenny added on a chuckle.

Lauren glared at her friend. 'I don't think so, thank you very much.'

'Oh, dear. Do I sense a falling out? And I had such high hopes for the two of you.'

'Haven't you got some cupboard to tidy out?' Lauren suggested.

Jenny looked at her knowingly but decided not to pursue things further. Lauren would tell her what was wrong when she was good and ready.

In her office, Lauren decided she could wait no longer for the estate agent to call her and she called him. Might as well get it over with.

'Ah, Dr Fletcher. I was just going to call you. I've spoken to the vendors of Abby's Cottage and they are prepared to accept your offer. The curtains and carpets are extra, of course, and there are several other pieces they thought might interest you.'

Trevor's words were music to her ears!

'That's wonderful!' she said, beaming. 'Great. I'll have to think about any extras. My budget's a bit tight. But we can discuss all that later. I'm so pleased. I thought someone else might make a better offer.'

'Well, Dr Asprey was very keen but

when he saw your interest, he decided to withdraw.'

'Really? That was very decent of him.' She was genuinely surprised. But perhaps his wife had decided it was unsuitable.

'If you give me the name of your solicitors, I'll get things moving. The vendors are looking for a quick completion. I believe you said that's what you want, too?'

'Oh yes. The sooner the better. I'll call into your office later with all my details.'

As Lauren almost danced out to find Jenny and share the good news, she crashed right into the arms of Tom Asprey.

'Lauren!' he gasped. 'Have I missed some emergency?'

'No . . . I'm sorry. I mean . . . well . . . I was just . . . I've got the cottage. They've accepted my offer.'

'That's terrific. Congratulations. It's certainly a lovely little place. I'll admit I was very tempted but I could see it was just perfect for you.'

'Yes, it is. Well, sorry about crashing into you. I must get on.'

She extracted herself from his arms which she'd realised were still resting around her waist far too comfortably. She pushed him gently away, fighting every urge not to. Her legs were beginning to feel weak. It was ridiculous!

'Lauren, please. Let me explain . . . ' he began.

'There's nothing to explain. Excuse me — things to do.'

She fled down the corridor towards the children's ward with nothing in mind other than to escape from him. She couldn't trust herself to be near him. Clearly she shouldn't trust him either.

The ward sister was sitting at her desk while most of the children were having their afternoon nap or reading.

'Lauren! To what do we owe this pleasure? Tom's only just left us after his rounds.'

'Oh, sorry, has he? I didn't realise. Everyone OK?'

'Fine thanks.'

She walked between the beds, smiling at the children and stopping to chat to one or two who were awake.

'How are you today Patrick?' she asked the little boy with asthma.

'I'm much better. Dr Tom says I can probably go home tomorrow. He's nice, isn't he?'

'Very nice,' Lauren agreed.

'He likes you,' Patrick confided. 'I asked him if he did and he said yes.'

'Really? Well, he couldn't really say anything else, could he? We work together all the time.'

'Do you like him too?'

'Of course I do. Now, settle down for your sleep or Sister will be after both of us for disturbing the peace.' She patted his hand. 'Get some rest now and I'll see you later.'

She gave him a wave as she left the ward, wondering where she could hide herself next — anything to avoid another confrontation with Tom.

It was such a ridiculous situation. She knew she should face up to him and resume a sensible, working relationship, but she wasn't ready yet. She needed to control the pounding in her chest every time she saw him, and stop herself from feeling faint every time he touched her, however casually.

How could someone casually brushing her arm make her feel so special? Especially a *married* someone, with a child. Curse the man, she muttered as she swept along the corridor.

* * *

'I've made you some coffee,' Jenny announced as she arrived back in the emergency department. 'You looked like you need it. It's in your office.'

'That's very kind of you. Thanks. Hey, guess what? I've got the cottage. My offer was accepted.'

'Oh, Lauren, that's brilliant! Well done. Congratulations on joining the mortgaged-up-to-the-hilt brigade. So, Dr Tom dropped out, did he?'

'Apparently. Probably not big enough for him and his . . . family.'

'His family? You mean . . . ?'

'Yes. Wife and child. Didn't you know?' She tried very hard to sound casual.

'Oh, love, I'm sorry. I was so tactless. I could see you were attracted to him and — well, him to you. What a disappointment.'

Right on cue, the disappointment came into the office.

'So this is where you're hiding. Any of that coffee left?'

'Sure,' Lauren said casually. 'Help yourself.'

As he reached over for the pot and poured himself a cup, his arm brushed against her shoulder. Unsuccessfully, she steeled herself to feel nothing.

'I guess I'd better go and check on the hoards out there,' Jenny said, glancing at the pair of doctors. 'I'll need you in a minute, Lauren, when you've finished your coffee.'

Lauren smiled and nodded. Jenny had obviously picked up on her discomfort.

'So, how does it feel to be a property owner?' Tom asked, aware of the frostiness in the air.

'Not quite an owner yet. But I'm working on it. That reminds me, I have to find myself a solicitor and give a name to the estate agent. Excuse me, will you? I'd better make some calls then get out to see whatever it is Jenny needs me for.'

She grabbed the phone book and began to search for the name of a local solicitor, but the words danced before her eyes and she could see nothing.

She felt Tom's eyes studying her and she blushed under the scrutiny.

'Lauren, we need to talk,' he said softly. 'Please let me explain.'

'Sure. I may have a slot next week sometime.' She shelved the directory. 'I think I'd better leave this for now. It's not fair to leave Jenny to cope alone.'

Flustered, she left him sitting in their shared office.

Lauren was furious with herself. Where on earth was the cool, cope-with-anything Dr Fletcher when she needed her? The current inhabitant of her body was more like an agitated teenage twit, nursing a crush on a forbidden man instead of the intelligent doctor she was supposed to be.

'I was just about to call you,' Jenny said. 'There's an elderly man coming in. He's had a fall and the ambulance crew thought we ought to check him out. Nothing broken, they reckon, but all the same . . . '

'OK. What's their ETA?'

'Five minutes.'

She went into one of the cubicles and prepared the bed, checking the oxygen supply and various pieces of equipment she might need. It wasn't strictly necessary as the nursing staff always ensured that everything was in order, but it helped her to re-focus. Hearing the doors from the ambulance bay swish open, she stepped forward to welcome her patient.

'This is Mr Graham Forbes,' the paramedic told her. 'He had a tumble in his hallway and couldn't manage to get up again. His wife called us out. He hit his head too so we thought we should get him checked over.'

'Hello, Mr Forbes. I'm Dr Fletcher,' Lauren said to her patient, an elderly man who looked pale and shaken. 'We're going to put you on this bed and take a look at you — see what we need to do for you, OK?'

The man looked dejected. 'I'm sorry to cause so much trouble. It was silly of me — I thought I'd manage to get to the door without my Zimmer frame. I just hope my Maisie's all right.'

'Is Maisie your wife? Is she here with you?'

'No. I told her to stay at home. We've got a little cat, you see. If Maisie left her, there'd be nobody to feed her, would there?'

Tom popped his head into the

cubicle at that moment. 'Need any help?'

'I can manage, thanks,' Lauren assured him. 'Though you can take a corner if you like and help lift Mr Forbes over. OK, everyone? One, two, three . . .'

The man gasped as he touched down on the bed.

'Oh! I seem to have hurt my hip. It didn't hurt before but when I landed on the bed — oh my!' He closed his eyes and paled as the pain swept over him.

'We'll take a look and give you something to ease the pain. Can we get bloods and fluids to the lab, please?' Lauren called out. 'Tom, maybe you could take a look at his head wound. Have you got pain anywhere else Mr Forbes? Mr Forbes?'

There was no reply.

'He's arrested! Get the crash trolley,' Tom shouted. 'We'll have to shock him.'

Paula brought the equipment immediately and the next few minutes flashed past in a blur with everyone concentrating on playing their part to bring the man back to life.

'We've got him,' Lauren announced with relief. 'Pulse faint but steady. Mr Forbes? Mr Forbes! Can you hear me?'

His eyes flicked open and he murmured something. Nobody could be sure but it sounded faintly like 'Maisie'.

'Should I phone his wife?' Jenny whispered.

Tom raised a questioning eyebrow at Lauren, who gave a slight shrug. It was a difficult choice. It was only fair that the old man should have his wife at his bedside, but if she was equally frail it might be too much for her. They could easily end up with two patients.

'I could see if the paramedics who brought him in are still around,' said Jenny. 'They could give us a picture of the home circumstances.'

'Good thinking,' Tom agreed and Jenny went to look for them.

The two doctors worked on the patient until they were happy that he was stabilised. They made a good team, each anticipating the other's needs and working in perfect harmony.

At last they reached the point when they knew they could leave him to the nursing staff until he was moved to the high dependency ward.

'Thank you.' Tom smiled at her as they left the room. 'I'm sorry if I intruded on your case.'

'It's a good job you did or we might have lost him,' she replied.

'Perfect teamwork, I'd say. I wonder if Jenny managed to contact his wife?'

'I'll find her and ask,' Lauren said, glad of something positive to do.

'She's pretty frail herself,' Jenny told her when they met up. 'The guys decided to leave her at home, and I think that may be best on the whole. I'll phone and tell her that her husband will have to stay in for a few days, and I can try to find out if there's someone who could be with her.'

'Good. She'll probably need some support, and the shock of this will be enough for her to cope with. Do you know where she lives?'

'Over near Redmore village. It's pretty much in the middle of nowhere, I gather.'

'Well, see how you get on and maybe I'll call in on my way home.'

Jenny shook her head at her. 'I'm sure there's no need for that. And it's hardly on your way home — I'll get social services onto it.'

'I don't like to think of a poor old lady being isolated somewhere with no-one to help or care for her,' Lauren protested.

'Lauren Fletcher, you're a lovely, kind, idiotic fool.' Jenny smiled. 'If you have time, could you look in on maternity? Joanne called for someone to check on a patient when there was anyone free. She's not too worried but the labour has been going on for some time.'

'OK,' Lauren agreed. 'I'll go over there now, as long as everything's covered here. Tom will go and check on

Mr Forbes, I expect.'

She went down the maze of corridors to the small maternity unit. The young mother-to-be was the only patient.

'Thanks for coming down, Lauren,' Joanne, the midwife, said. 'I just want someone to take a look at Sally here. It's her first baby and she's been in labour for about ten hours now. Everything seems OK but I want to be sure . . . '

Lauren checked the patient's details and her ante-natal reports.

'How are you doing? How's the pain? Not too much for you?' she asked the young girl.

'S'all right. Me mum said it would hurt but it isn't too bad yet. Can I have something to help if it gets worse?'

'Of course you can. Just ask. Isn't there anyone you'd like to have with you?'

'Nah. Me mum's got the other kids to look after and my husband's gone away on the fishing boats. We weren't sure exactly when it was due, to be honest. He did offer to stay on shore this time but we need the money. Nice surprise when he gets back.'

Lauren was surprised too. The girl looked too young to have a husband. But then, she looked too young to be having a baby, too.

'You're very brave. Good girl. Don't worry, Jo here will take good care of you. Call me if you need me,' she added to Jo.

'Thanks, Lauren. How are things with you?' Jo asked. 'I hear you've got a dishy new boss. I haven't met him yet. What's he like?'

'Very nice. A good doctor. Knows his stuff.'

'And dishy?'

'I suppose it depends on your taste.'

'Any male who breathes and is under forty will suit me,' Joanne joked. 'I could do with being taken off the shelf, if only for a light dusting.'

'You should come out for a drink with all of us one evening. We usually go once a month or so. Then you can meet him for yourself.'

'Thanks. I'd like that. I'm a bit isolated out here. Thanks for coming down. I expect Sally will be fine but I'll give you a shout if I need you.'

★ ★ ★

When she returned to the department, Lauren was relieved to find that Tom was still occupied. She knew she needed to face up to the situation very soon but she still felt too foolish, too hurt.

She glanced over her desk to see if there were any messages and saw that attached to the computer monitor was a sticker with the name and number of a solicitor. There was no signature but she recognised Tom's scrawl. There was also a single cross at the bottom. A kiss? How dared he? All the same, she was glad of the address and appreciated the time it had saved. She dialled the number.

'Hoskins and Willoughby,' said a

bored sounding receptionist.

'May I speak to Mr Hoskins?'

After several questions and a growing impatience from Lauren, she was finally put through.

'Hello, Dr Fletcher. This is David Hoskins. You're a friend of Tom's, I gather?'

'Er — yes. Well, we work together. I didn't realise you know him.'

'We were at school together. Lost touch over the years, but when he called, we arranged to have a drink later. Will you be coming along?'

'No, I'm sorry, I assumed he'd simply looked in the phone directory and found you. I'm buying a house and need someone to act for me.'

'No problem. I'll just take a few details . . .'

After the call was finished, Lauren realised she felt irritated. She'd thought Tom had merely been trying to save her some time — not organising meetings with one of his old cronies.

'Oh, good — you found the phone

number,' Tom said as he came into the office. 'I looked through the book and couldn't believe it when I saw Dave Hoskins' name there. I'd forgotten he came from this part of the world. Coincidence, eh? Was he any use to you?'

'Yes, thanks.'

'You could come with me to meet him this evening if you like.'

'You must have a very understanding wife — with you always going out,' she snapped.

'You don't know anything about my wife,' he retorted, looking slightly puzzled.

'Of course I don't. You chose not to tell me.'

With that she rushed out of the office, knowing that if she stayed she would either have a dreadful row with him or burst into tears. She had to push him away when what she wanted most of all was to draw him close to her and feel his arms around her. The look in his eyes could melt her bones to liquid with just one glance.

It was much too dangerous to be anywhere near him. Until she had managed to rebuild her usual stout protective shield around her heart, she must avoid being alone with him and work at trying to see him as nothing more than a friendly colleague.

At the end of the day, she looked through the records and made a note of Mrs Forbes's address. Though it probably wasn't very professional of her, she didn't like the thought of the old lady sitting alone. Jenny was nowhere around so she couldn't check whether she'd managed to contact anyone for her.

Before she left, she went to visit Mr Forbes. They had decided to retain him in the high dependency unit overnight to keep a closer check on him.

'Hello, Mr Forbes. It's Dr Fletcher. I saw you when you first came in. How are you feeling now?'

'Oh, hello, Dr Fletcher. My, I'm getting first class treatment. That other doctor's just been in to see me as well. I'm feeling fine — thank you for asking. Just a bit wobbly. But I'm worried about my Maisie. We've never been apart, you see, not once since we were married. She won't like being on her own.'

'Haven't you got any family who could stay with her?'

'Our son's in America. Doing very well, he is. But it's a long way away. And he's very busy.' The old man closed his eyes wearily.

'Don't worry, someone will go and visit your wife to make sure she's all right.'

'Thank you. I don't want her to worry. You're all very kind, I must say. It's nice to be in this hospital. I was afraid they'd send me all the way to Truro.'

Lauren smiled. 'See you in the morning.'

Getting To Know Jake

As she drove out to the tiny hamlet where the Forbeses lived, Lauren reflected on the sadness of the old couple, separated for the first time and both of them sick and frail. They'd obviously had a good, long life together.

She couldn't stifle a sigh. Even if she managed to find the right man now, she'd be almost eighty by the time they'd shared fifty years.

She glanced down at the address on the seat beside her and made the turn into a narrow lane. There was a car parked outside the little cottage. She sighed. That meant she would have to back out again or go and disturb the person to ask him to move his car.

She stared. There was something familiar about that car . . .

'Oh no,' she breathed. It was Tom's car. What on earth was he doing here?

She couldn't help but smile. It was quite obvious what he was doing — he was visiting the old lady, just as she was. Well, there was no point in her going into the cottage with him there. Leave Tom to it, she decided.

She reversed along the lane and back on to the road. At least now she had time to call at the supermarket and stock up her store cupboard.

She glanced down to make sure her pager was switched on. She had checked with Jo before she left and told the midwife to beep her if she wanted any help.

She drove back to town and did her shopping, still feeling as if she were in limbo, as if she was waiting for something to happen.

It was quite ridiculous and illogical. She'd always found plenty to do in the evenings but now she simply felt bored.

Perhaps some of the staff were out having a drink, she thought suddenly, brightening a little.

She drove past their regular pub and

looked to see if there were any cars she recognised, but the car park was virtually empty. So there was nothing else for it but to have a quiet night at home in front of the television. Or she could always go and take another peek at her cottage, she thought. Just from the outside, of course.

Her cottage. It gave her a warm glow to think of it like that.

She drove quickly to the next village and stopped outside the cottage.

It looked so perfect. Roses round the door, contrasting with the grey Cornish granite. She peered over the wall into the tiny front garden. She would put stones down there and have tubs of bright flowers. She could see that it needed quite a lot of work doing, but nothing concerned her about that. This would be her home, however long it took to sort out and pay for. Feeling happier at last, she drove home.

Jo called her the next morning to announce that Sally had delivered a girl. There had been no problems and both were doing well.

'She'll be a good mum, however young she is,' Jo told her. 'Some have just got it, haven't they?'

'Yes. Thanks for letting me know. Give her my congratulations.'

Lucky girl, Lauren thought. She was happy with her lot. Pity we're not all so easily satisfied, she told herself.

★　★　★

The days passed quickly. She and Tom seemed to have developed the working relationship she'd been striving for. Though her heart was still behaving irrationally whenever they were alone together, at least he seemed to have accepted that anything between them was over — not that there had been much in the first place. Obviously he did have a conscience after all. That was the trouble with working in an emergency department, emotions always seemed to run higher than anywhere else.

'Mr Forbes is going home tomorrow,' he told her one morning. 'I've managed to find some temporary help for them at home, and social services are going to come up with something more permanent. Maisie's quite a sweetie.'

'Have you been visiting her?'

'Well, I know it isn't strictly the right thing to do, but, yes, I called round once or twice.'

She smiled. 'I thought so. Actually. I went round too. I saw your car parked so I thought I'd leave you to it.'

'I see. So Dr Fletcher doesn't have a heart of stone after all?'

'Never did have. In fact, it's a heart that's inclined to be rather too mushy, so I have to put a cage round it for protection.'

Smiling, she left him to deal with the emergencies and went off to do her rounds.

She felt pleased with herself. She'd managed a normal conversation instead of scurrying out of the room the moment he'd arrived.

It was a good day. Things were running smoothly and the queues were manageable most of the time.

A group of them went out for a drink after work and when she finally got back to her flat, she felt more content than she had for several days. She cooked some supper and settled down with her book. Perhaps she was getting over him.

'I'm going to make it, Ted,' she said, hugging her old friend. 'Even if I have gone potty and I'm talking to a stuffed toy!' She yawned and decided on an early night.

★ ★ ★

The hospital waiting-room was packed the following day. They opened at eight-thirty officially, but when Lauren came in at eight o' clock, there was already a long queue forming.

'What on earth was going on last night?' she demanded of Jenny as they eyed the queue.

'The local footie team won and the celebrations got out of hand,' Jenny told her.

'So why didn't they go to their GPs or to Truro?' Lauren asked.

'You know Landris — this is their local hospital and they want to use it, even if it means waiting overnight. I'd better get out there and sort out who's in the worst state. Are you ready for the first ones?'

'I guess so. Where's Tom this morning?'

'I don't know. There's no sign of him yet. Your first customer's in cubicle two. He's bleeding all over the place. I had to separate him from the rest — he's still suffering something of a hangover.'

'Great. I hope security are around. I might need them before today's out. Some of them still seem to be celebrating, by the sound of it.' She grimaced and went out to start work.

'Now then,' she said to her first patient, 'let's take a look at your hand. I'm Dr Fletcher . . .'

The routine speeches and words of comfort continued throughout the morning as she swabbed, stitched, injected and passed the minor injuries patients on to the nurses. By midday she felt exhausted.

'Any chance of a coffee?' she called out to anyone listening. 'And what's happening with Tom? Anyone made contact?'

'Some domestic crisis, I gather. He's on his way now.'

'What do you have to do to get service around here?' grumbled a large angry-looking woman from the queue. 'We've been waiting for hours. That lot came in ages after us and they got seen to right away.'

'I'm sorry, madam,' Lauren placated her. 'We have to take the most serious cases first. But if you'd like to come this way, I'll see you now.' So much for a five-minute break and her caffeine fix, she thought.

'It's my husband. He's been feeling sick all night and now he's got a headache.' The woman dragged an unhappy looking man behind her as she spoke. 'Now sit down, our Jack. Let the doctor take a look at you.'

Five minutes later, Lauren sent them away having decided it was no more than mild food poisoning, probably due to having eaten two large pork pies that were well past their use by date. She'd suggested that a visit to their own GP would have saved them the waiting time, but the woman had not taken the criticism kindly.

'We pays our taxes for this hospital so we've got every right to use it,' she called out on her way out.

'Tom's just arrived — with a miniature version of himself,' Jenny told Lauren when she saw she was free. 'They're in the office.'

Lauren went to look for them and found Tom looking very strained.

'Lauren, I'm so sorry. Our au pair's ill and had to go home to her mum. It's nothing serious but I couldn't refuse. It also happens to be some sort of training day at Jake's school so he's got the day off. I spent half the morning trying to find someone to look after him but, as you can see, failed miserably. This is Jake, by the way.'

'Hi, Jake. Nice to meet you.' Her mind was whirling. His au pair? Not his wife?

'Hello.' Jake held out a small hand for her to shake. 'Are you a doctor as well?'

'Yes. I'm Lauren.'

'I've seen you before,' he went on. 'When we went to look at a house that Daddy wanted to buy.'

'That's right. But I didn't have time to stop to speak to you then.'

'We liked the cottage. Daddy said we couldn't buy it though 'cos you wanted it very much.'

'That was very thoughtful of him. I didn't realise. I thought it was just too small for you all.'

Tom grinned. 'Always thoughtful, that's us. Now, Jake, what are we going to do with you for the rest of the day? Do you think you could sit in the office quietly and do some drawing? If Dr Fletcher doesn't mind, that is?'

'That's fine by me,' she put in. 'He could even go along to the children's ward later and play with some of the toys there. There's no-one infectious there just now.'

'Great idea. You'd have to play quietly though, sport. Some of the children are pretty sick and we wouldn't want them to get too excited. But there are lots of toys there and you might find someone who'd like to play with you.'

'That would be nice. I can be very, very quiet — you know I can.' Jake looked very earnest and Lauren's heart was totally captured.

'Shall we go and see if it's all right with Sister?' Lauren offered.

The child slipped a trusting hand into hers and they set off down the long corridor. He chatted all the way, telling her about Sophie being sick and crying because she felt so unwell.

He quickly settled down at a table in

the ward with various toys. One of the other boys went to sit with him and, in the way of children, you'd have thought they'd known each other for ages as they instantly got a game organised.

'Thanks,' Lauren said to Sister. 'I know it's a bit of an imposition but it is an emergency. Call one of us if you need anything.'

She glanced at her watch. It was well after one and she was starving.

Buying a sandwich and a packet of crisps from the snack bar, she took them back to the office.

She felt so much happier now she knew that Jake's mother wasn't the pretty girl who looked far too young to be the mother of a six-year-old. All the same, there must be — or have been — a mother somewhere. Perhaps Tom was a widower. If that was the case, she had cruelly misjudged him. She felt a pang of guilt for the way she had reacted.

'Have you eaten?' she asked Tom, who was leafing through the pile of morning reports.

'Yes, thanks. I grabbed something for us both before I left. I say, you must have been frantic this morning. I'm so sorry.'

'It was a bit hairy at times, but we coped. Too many of our patients seem to have an aversion to their G.P.s.

'I can't think why. We don't really have that problem at home. Sorry, in New Zealand. But then, we have Medicare and payment could be a factor, I guess. G.P.s come cheaper than hospitals.'

'What made you leave?'

'Long story.' His eyes clouded for a moment and he drew breath to speak again — just as the phone rang. 'I'll get it. You deserve a break. Eat your lunch before you collapse. Hello?' he said into the receiver.

Lauren listened to his side of the conversation.

'OK — got that. You're kidding! Not again! OK — one of us will come right away — probably me but I'll discuss it with my colleague. OK — give precise directions to the nurse while I sort out the gear.'

He grimaces as he put the phone down. 'Seems there's another rescue call. Don't people value their lives around here?'

'It is the holiday season,' she pointed out, 'so that means there are more people about.'

'All the more reason to take care if you're a holiday-maker and don't know the area, I'd have thought,' said Tom.

'Do you want me to go? You've only just got here.'

'I'm happy to go. It's just — there's Jake.' He bit his lip anxiously. 'You've been on the go all morning so you're bound to be tired, and if there's climbing involved again . . .'

'You go. I'll take care of Jake. He doesn't seem to mind being with strangers.'

'He's used to it. OK — thanks. Needs must.' He put a hand on her shoulder and squeezed gently. She smiled up at him and touched his hand with hers.

'No problem. Now get on your way. Call if you need help.'

* * *

Once Tom had left, there were no patients waiting, so Lauren did the ward rounds. Though other doctors visited the wards, in such a relatively small hospital it was part of her duty to keep a check on them, particularly on patients who'd been admitted through the emergency department.

She spoke to an elderly farmer who was making good progress on his angina medication. His hand wound was also healing well. He would soon be home again.

Finally she went to the children's ward where she found Jake sitting with a cup of milk and a cake on a plate beside him.

'Sister said I could have tea with the others since I'm a visitor. I did say thank you very much.' His large eyes looked up anxiously, a mirror image of the look in his father's eyes just a short time ago.

'I'm sure you did. Have you had a good time?'

'Yes, thank you. Where's my daddy?'

'He's had to go out on an emergency call. I don't suppose he'll be too long, but don't worry, I'm looking out for you till he gets back. Now, are you OK while I make my rounds? I have to see some of the children here to check they're all behaving and taking their medicine.'

'I know. Daddy told me all about it. I'm fine. Thank you for looking out for me.'

'You're welcome, Jake.'

'Proper little charmer, isn't he?' Sister said. 'Just like his father. So polite. But he looks scared half to death in case he does something wrong. I expect his dad's put the fear of God into him if he misbehaves.'

'That doesn't sound like Tom. He's

quite a gentle soul really. Now, how's everyone doing?'

They went from bed to bed, discussing progress, medications and checking dressings. Lauren wrote up any changes and chatted to her small charges.

'Everything perfectly in order as always, Sister,' she said with satisfaction when she had finished. 'And thanks again for taking Jake under your wing.'

'Leave him here till Tom gets back if you like. I know A and E can be a bit fraught at times.'

'Thanks, but we're quiet at the moment — or at least we were when I left. Thank goodness! I could do with some peace after this morning's rush. I've got some paperwork to catch up on, so I can sit in the office with him, for the time being anyhow.'

Jake sat drawing and writing little captions beneath his pictures. Nowhere did his mother feature. There were pictures of Cornwall with sea and cliffs and some of New Zealand with tree ferns called pungas.

Lauren looked anxiously at her watch. It was after six and there was still no news of Tom and his emergency call-out. Jenny and Paula were ready to go and were hovering in the reception area.

'It's OK, you go. I'll wait on for Tom,' Lauren told them. 'There's someone on the main desk all the time, so I don't need to worry about being on my own. Besides, I've always got Jake to look after me.'

She smiled at the boy and he came and slipped his hand into hers. She hoisted him on to her knee and liked the unfamiliar feel of his little body against her own. He yawned and leaned against her.

'Are you tired?' she asked him.

'Yes. We didn't get much sleep last night with Sophie chucking up everywhere. Whoops — I'm not supposed to say that. Injectile vomiting, Daddy says.'

'Projectile vomiting I think you mean,' Lauren said, stifling a laugh.

Trust a doctor to make his child use the accurate term. 'Look, how about we go back to my house and we can get something to eat? It's not far away and we can leave a message here for your dad so's he knows where we are.'

'That would be nice. Have you moved into that cottage yet?'

'Not yet. It takes ages to buy a house. I still live in my flat. It's very small but I won't be staying there for much longer.'

She quickly scribbled a note for Tom, adding her phone number and the address in case he had lost them. She gave it to the receptionist in the main entrance. He was on duty all night so would see everyone who came and went.

'Have you had any news about the call-out?' she asked him. 'They've been gone a long time.'

'Nothing yet. I reckon he's probably gone straight to Truro with the crew. Probably waiting for a lift back.'

'Maybe. Well, I'll get this young man home and we'll wait and see. 'Night, George.'

'Good night, Dr Fletcher.'

Jake held her hand tightly as they walked to her flat. It was only about ten minutes but she could tell he was tired out.

'Not much farther,' she promised. 'If I'd known I was going to have a visitor, I'd have brought my car to work. What shall we have for tea? Do you like pasta?'

'I like it the way my dad cooks it. He makes it all tomato saucy. With cheese on top.'

'I think we can probably manage that. And even some ice cream for pudding. Does that sound OK?'

'Excellent,' he said, striding out with a little more enthusiasm.

Lauren made the sauce, chatting to Jake as she did so. He seemed more at ease now he was away from the hospital and tentatively she probed for a little more information.

'Do you like living in Cornwall?' she began.

'I think so. I liked New Zealand but

there were problems.'

'I see. What do you mean — at school? Or Daddy's work?'

'I'm — I'm not s'posed to talk about it,' he replied hesitantly.

'I'm sorry. I didn't mean to be nosy. You don't have to talk about anything you don't want to.'

'It's all right. You're a friend, aren't you? Not just one of Daddy's colly — colly things.'

'Colleague?' Lauren suggested and the boy nodded.

'Do you want to tell me about it?' she asked gently.

'Yes, please. But you won't tell anyone else, will you?'

'Of course not. But don't tell me anything that you should keep secret.' She paused. 'Is it something to do with your mum?'

Tears filled his eyes and instinctively she went to put her arms round him. But he shrank back as if avoiding her touch.

'Hey, it's OK,' she assured him

gently, and felt him relax and nestle against her. She felt tears prick her own eyes.

'Did your mum . . . die?'

He shook his head. 'No,' he whispered. 'She's still at home. But they kept shouting at each other all the time. Well, not always. And then Tanya got cross and shouted at me. Daddy decided we might be better living somewhere else. And . . . and . . . ' He broke off as a huge sob made him gulp.

'I think this sauce must be just about ready. Can you give it a stir while I put on the pasta?' Lauren's mind was whirling. It didn't sound like Tom to shout at anyone. But, then, she didn't really know him very well, did she, and nothing was ever quite what it seemed.

Distracting Jake seemed the best course of action and she kept him stirring the sauce while she grated cheese and cooked the pasta.

'Do you mind if I wait till your dad comes back before I eat mine? He'll be hungry and we could eat together.'

'OK. It'll be nicer for Daddy as well.'

She smiled and spooned out a plateful for the child.

He ate hungrily and seemed to approve of her cooking . . . He certainly finished every last mouthful.

'Your pasta's better than Dad's but you'd better not tell him I said so. It might hurt his feelings.'

He gave a huge yawn and Lauren noticed he was looking rather pale.

'Would you like to go to bed in my room? If you have a bit of a sleep you might feel better. I don't know how much longer your dad's going to be but we can wake you after he's had something to eat.'

'Yes, please. I do feel very sleepy. Is that your teddy bear?'

'It is. His name's Ted. You could take him with you to keep you company if you like.'

'My mum said I was too big for toys and that was a long time ago. Do you think it matters if I take him with me?'

'Of course not. He's very good at

cuddling people when they feel a bit tired or unhappy.'

He smiled and picked up the elderly bear. Soon, both boy and bear were snuggled down under the duvet and Jake fell asleep in seconds.

* * *

A short time later, she heard a knock at the door. A white-faced Tom stood outside.

'You look all in,' she said. 'Come on in and sit down. Jake's asleep and I've got some pasta waiting for you.'

'You're a saviour. Why do these things all have to happen at once?'

She poured them each some wine and they sat together on her sofa.

'So what happened? Why are you so late?'

'A couple — holiday-makers — had got cut off by the tide. We climbed round intending to lead them back, but the woman got all het up and ended up having a full-blown panic attack. The paramedics were there and we managed to calm her. But naturally we couldn't do anything dramatic on the ground, so we had to call the air ambulance. Well, to cut it short, I eventually ended up at Truro and I've only just got back.'

'Are they OK?'

'Yes. He's broken his ankle but it could have been worse. That's two similar accidents in just a few weeks.'

'You can expect a couple more at least, and probably even some drownings,' Lauren warned him. 'It's sad but true. Now, sit still and I'll get us something to eat.'

She busied herself in the tiny kitchen and quickly produced two heaped plates of steaming food.

'Wow, this is wonderful! Thanks so much. I bet Jake enjoyed his. This is his favourite.'

She grinned. 'So I gathered! He gave me very precise instructions.'

They ate hungrily and Lauren felt relaxed. She was intrigued to learn more about this man and his reasons for leaving his adopted country.

She took a deep breath and took the plunge.

'Jake was talking a bit about leaving New Zealand.'

'Really?' he said in some surprise. 'He doesn't usually want to talk about it at all. It was a very difficult time. My . . . my wife had become unwell. She didn't cope with things and us leaving the country altogether seemed like a good idea at the time.'

'Sounds a bit dramatic. Was she a local girl?'

'Yes. We married fairly soon after I emigrated. I went out there right after I was qualified. My parents had both died. It didn't seem there was anything to keep me here. Jake was born a year after we married. I guess there were mistakes on both sides, but that didn't excuse her behaviour.'

'You don't have to tell me this if you don't want to,' Lauren began.

'No, I do want to tell you.' He ran his fingers through his already tousled hair.

'I've been wanting to tell you everything since that first evening. You must realise how I feel about you. Don't you believe in love at first sight?'

She gasped.

'Love? That's a bit strong, isn't it? You know nothing about me.'

'Not yet, but I hope to know everything about you one day, very soon.' His voice was soft and sincere as he moved to pull her into his arms, but Lauren shrank back.

'Tom, no, please!'

'I thought . . . I know you have feelings for me. I can see it in your lovely eyes.'

'But you're still married. Aren't you?' she asked, her eyes dark with emotion.

He nodded.

'Then this can't go anywhere. Not if you're not free.'

'But I will be. I have every intention of divorcing my wife as soon as possible. I've left her and moved to another continent, for heaven's sake. Doesn't that tell you anything? The divorce is virtually guaranteed.'

'But until then, I can't . . . please, Tom. You're tired and probably over-wrought. Can't we be friends? Just friends for now? If something more develops, that's great. But until then, please don't make things any more difficult than they are.' She wrung her hands. 'We do have to work together. Very closely. I can't cope with the strain. I . . . I'll go and make some coffee.'

Tom leaned back against the soft cushions. He closed his eyes and all he could see was Lauren's lovely face. He could smell her perfume on the cushions. She filled his senses. But there was Tanya looming between them. The familiar feeling rose within him as he recalled her moods, her cruelty. He still found it so hard to believe he could have married someone who would harm a child — any child, let alone her own little boy.

In the kitchen, Lauren automatically boiled the kettle and set out the mugs.

Her mind was full of Tom and the words he had spoken. How could she even consider any sort of relationship with him while he was still married? He may be planning to get a divorce but the fact remained, he was not free.

He was certainly charming and very attractive — in fact, he was everything she'd ever dreamed of finding. He was wonderful with people and obviously a very good father. Thinking about it, though, Jake did have a nervousness about him and was obviously terrified of making any mistakes. She didn't know enough about Tom — or about any of it

There was more, much more she needed to know before she could make any sort of judgement. He had run away from New Zealand and turned his back on his marriage. If he'd done it once, wouldn't he be quite capable of doing it again? If he could walk out on a marriage, he could easily leave a mere girlfriend if he wanted to. She daren't, couldn't risk that sort of hurt. Once was enough in anyone's life.

But the thudding of her heart was contradicting the sense that her mind was trying to tell her — Tom was her dream man in every way.

She carried the tray into the sitting-room, where she stopped short — Tom was sprawled out on her sofa, fast asleep. His dark eyelashes lay on his cheeks, hiding the weary look she'd seen in his eyes. She longed to touch his hair, tousled as it often was.

She picked up a throw from the armchair and laid it over him. He must be exhausted.

There was only one problem now. Where was she going to sleep? Jake was tucked up in her bed and Tom occupied the sofa. She'd have to make do with the chair, a pillow and a blanket.

She crept into the bedroom. Jake was fast asleep, one arm flung over his head and the other clutching her old teddy. She touched the little head very gently and slipped the spare pillow from beside him.

She collected a blanket from the airing cupboard and made herself as comfortable as she could in the armchair, leaving just a small lamp alight in case either of them awoke. She looked at Tom. There was something very intimate about watching someone sleep. He looked so vulnerable, so like the small boy who slept, oblivious to everything, in the next room.

I could really fall in love with this man, she thought. *And his child*, she added. *Could* love? The feelings she had about him suggested she already did love him. The realisation stunned her. In all the years since Adam, she had never allowed herself to express such thoughts. Adam had seriously damaged her ability to trust anyone.

'Is There Any Hope?'

It was five-thirty when Lauren awoke with a start. She couldn't understand why she had a dreadful crick in her neck. She rubbed it and sat up as realisation came to her.

Tom was also sitting up, rubbing his own aching limbs. He smiled at her. 'I'm so sorry. I can't think what happened. I was chatting one minute and now I've only just come to. What time is it?'

'Half-past five. You needed the sleep. I gather you didn't get much sleep the night before, either.' She told him about Jake's description and Tom laughed deliciously.

They chatted for a few minutes, until Lauren decided they needed some coffee. As she rinsed out the coffee pot in the kitchen, she sensed Tom's presence behind her.

129

He put his hands on her shoulders and turned her towards him.

'Lauren, please tell me you think there could be a chance for us?'

'I don't know. Maybe,' she replied. 'But you know my terms. I can't think about it until you're divorced. It isn't fair to Jake. Or me. If you ran away from a marriage once, how do I know you won't run away from me too?'

Her voice shook slightly as she forced herself to deal with his closeness. His scent was filling her whole being and threatening to drown her. It was bliss — and torture to have to resist.

'Ran away? Is that what you think?' He sounded hurt. 'You don't understand. I didn't run away. It's a long and complicated story.'

'So, tell me.'

He drew in his breath to speak but he didn't manage to utter a word.

'Daddy. Where are you, Daddy?' called Jake. 'And where's Lauren? Why are we still here?'

'Hi, Jakey boy. Did you sleep well?'

'I can't remember so I suppose I did. Is it getting up time?'

There was no further opportunity to talk. They had toast and coffee and Tom took Jake back home to get ready for school.

Lauren was thoughtful. Maybe she was wrong to make judgements. Perhaps there was much more to hear. All the same, her basic premise was still there. She could not make any commitment to Tom until she felt more certain — and until his divorce was a fact.

She jogged the short distance to the hospital, hoping the exercise would loosen up her aching muscles. Chairs were simply not built for sleeping in and her legs felt stiff and cramped. It was a warm sunny day and looked like being hot later on. She changed into hospital scrubs, knowing the loose fitting garments would be cooler than a white coat over her clothes. The first trickle of patients were coming into the waiting-room and Jenny was already getting things ready.

'There's a little boy with a nasty scald on his foot. He's in cubicle three.' Jenny paused and looked more closely at Lauren. 'You look a bit the worse for wear. Heavy night?'

'Not exactly what you mean but I do feel pretty shattered.'

'Tom's not in yet. I gather he had a late call too. How did it go with his little boy?'

'Jake? Fine. He's gorgeous. Now, I'd better get to this scald.'

She examined the angry-looking red mark.

'How did it happen?' she asked the anxious mother.

'He grabbed my coffee cup and managed to tip it all over his foot. He was wearing slippers at the time and it held the heat in. I managed to get them off pretty well right away, but it was a second or two before I realised what he'd done. You can't leave them a minute, can you?'

She smiled at the child. 'You'll have to let your mum have her coffee in a cup in future and not your slippers, won't you?' She turned back to his mum. 'Anyhow, he looks OK now. Keep his foot open to the air for today and don't let him walk on it more than necessary. If you're worried, either bring him back here or see your GP.'

'Thank you. You've been very kind,' she said as she led him away.

When Lauren went into the office, she found Tom inside.

'I've poured you a coffee,' he said.

'Oh, thanks. I was just coming to collect a new batch of record sheets.'

'I thought you might need to sit down and take a look at this.' He handed her a copy of the local paper.

Landris Hospital Under Threat, shouted the headlines.

Lauren froze and quickly scanned the rest of the article.

The local hospital trust are considering the viability of keeping the small, all-purpose unit open. They are considering the advantages of moving all treatment to Truro to provide better, more up-to-date facilities and consolidate the service. The date for an inquiry will be announced later.

'Honestly!' she exploded. 'What do they know about it? We work flat out all day and they dare to question whether it's a resource that's needed?'

Tom shrugged. 'Maybe there's something in it. We don't have many modern facilities here. We can't do MRI scans or CT scans. The X-ray unit is bordering on the ancient and we can only do relatively minor ops.'

'You've only been here for five minutes — you can't make this sort of judgement. Think of all the local people who come in here for treatment. Ask them what *they* think. Some of them could die if they had to go all the way to Truro. Look at Graham Forbes . . . and the farmer with the cut hand. If we hadn't spotted that he was suffering from angina, he might never have made it. They have such a huge A&E department there, it's a case of get them through as fast as possible to cut down the queues and waiting times. Directives demand that everyone is seen in so many minutes, blah, blah, blah. If they got all of our patients as well, heaven knows what would happen.'

Lauren paused for breath. She was growing quite pink with anger. Then she noticed Tom's mouth twitching at the corners.

'You're winding me up, aren't you?' she accused him. 'You feel the same as I do about small local hospitals.'

'Of course I do. Back in New Zealand, the medics have more responsibility and we do more minor ops in the GPs' own practices — many more than here. But the sort of facility Landris provides is essential to meet the local needs. If you're organising a protest, count me in.'

★   ★   ★

Lauren's admiration for Tom's medical skills were growing. She watched him deal with difficult patients with a charm and patience quite rare in these pressured times. Many of the doctors were so hassled they could only give the minimum time possible. Strangely, though he never seemed to hurry, Tom managed to fit in just as many patients as any of the other doctors. It was a rare skill. He was also very quick to pick up on any less obvious symptoms.

However, just as they came to the end of a discussion about a patient, he turned to Lauren, looking at her intently. He couldn't bear to talk only about work when there was so much else he needed to say to her.

'I want you to think about us,' he said. 'Seriously. I can't bear to be this close to you all the time and not have any hope.'

'Oh, Tom. I do care about you and Jake. Very much. But I daren't let anything happen. Not yet.'

'What's made you so scared of men?'

She looked away, her fingers twisting nervously together. Was she ready to tell him about her past? Maybe it was time.

136

For both of them.

'I'll tell you when we have time to talk properly,' she said at last. 'We both need to talk, don't we? But not here. We could be interrupted at any moment.'

Right on cue, Jenny called out, 'Ambulance coming in. Five minutes.'

Both doctors leapt to their feet and went through to the treatment room, any personal conversation set aside as they swung into action.

The Truth About Tanya

'Aren't we due for a drink after work?' Paula said towards the end of the afternoon. 'We haven't been sociable for ages, and it is Friday.'

She did a quick round of the department and could only gather a few people who were free. Tom had rushed out earlier to collect Jake from school and had brought him back to wait in the office till the end of the shift. Apparently Sophie, the au pair, was still being cosseted by her mother and wouldn't be back until after the weekend, so Tom had to collect Jake each day; he had no babysitter to help him out. Jake didn't seem to mind. He was pleased to see Lauren again.

'It was nice at your flat,' he said as he took his coloured pencils out of his schoolbag. Jenny overheard and raised her eyebrows at Lauren.

'Jake and Tom came to my place last night,' Lauren explained. 'Tom was out so late at that rescue that poor Jake was falling asleep . . . and he took my Teddy to bed with him, didn't you, Jake?'

She felt herself blushing as she babbled on, trying to ensure that Jenny didn't get the wrong idea about the previous evening.

'No need to explain.' Jenny grinned. 'I always did think there was something between you two. It's obvious from the way you look at each other.'

Lauren put a warning finger to her lips and nodded towards Jake who was sitting at Tom's desk, drawing a picture.

'I'll see you later,' she said. 'You're joining us for a drink after work, aren't you?'

'Of course. My dearly beloved's working late tonight so it'll be a take-away for him when he finally returns to the fold.'

'Oh, do you mind if we ask Jo? The midwife?' Lauren asked. 'She gets a bit lonely, I gather — it's a bit isolated along there.'

'Sure. The more the merrier. I'll give her a call.'

In the end, there was a group of six who left work together to head to the pub. Tom looked longingly at them as he left, Jake's hand clutched tightly in his. The little boy turned to wave at Lauren.

'Will you come to the beach with us tomorrow?' he called. 'Dad says we can go and build a huge sandcastle. You could come and help.'

Lauren hesitated.

'Well, I don't know that I'm much good at sandcastles,' she began, acutely aware that everyone was listening.

'We could give you a lesson,' Jake assured her eagerly. 'Me and Dad are good at building sandcastles.'

'Maybe Lauren has something else she needs to do,' Tom put in diplomatically. 'But let's leave it for now. We can always phone her later and see if she's free.' He grinned. 'Give her time to think of an excuse.'

Lauren knew there was nothing she'd

like more than a day on the beach with this adorable child and his even more adorable father.

Everyone was watching her to see what she would say. The gossip would soon begin and she knew she — they — would be teased unmercifully if their colleagues thought there was something going on.

'I have to see about my house. I have an appointment with my solicitor in the morning,' she said. 'Thanks all the same.'

Tom took the hint and left.

'So, how's it going with Dr Tom?' Paula asked as everyone found a table and began to settle down. Her underlying meaning was quite clear, but Lauren wasn't prepared to enlightened her.

'Fine, thanks. He's a very good doctor. Now, what does everyone want to drink?' She grabbed her purse and stood up. It was worth buying the first round if only to get away from the speculation for a few minutes. They were a tightly-knit group and thrived on every scrap of gossip.

She knew she was blushing and wanted to gather her thoughts. She really hoped Tom would phone and repeat the invitation in private. She'd be happy to accept, once she'd been to sign the papers the solicitor had phoned her about.

The rest of the evening passed happily. Jo had joined them, delighted to be asked. Everyone was relaxed at the end of the working week. There was a whole different staff on duty at weekends and the doctors took turns to give emergency cover about once a month. It worked well and meant that no-one was consistently overworked. They chatted about the weekend ahead but most of the conversation revolved around the possible closure of their hospital. They all agreed that a protest must be organised.

The evening stretched out, so that it was almost ten when Lauren finally reached her flat. She felt exhausted after the previous night's lack of sleep and went straight to bed, not noticing that her answering machine was flashing with a message.

★   ★   ★

When she finally played the message the next morning, Tom's voice filled the room.

'Hi, Lauren. Sorry about Jake's rather obvious invitation. I hope you weren't too embarrassed by him. I just wanted to thank you again for your help yesterday and to say that if you do feel like joining us tomorrow, we'd be delighted to have you along. I guess you're not back yet. I'll call again tomorrow. I'm offering you pasties for lunch.'

She smiled. Of course she would go. Had there ever been any doubt? However tough it was to resist the man, she wanted to be with him more than anything. She knew she was probably being over-cautious. She realised that she'd built a heavily-armed fortress around herself, rather than a mere protective shell. Perhaps it was time she opened a door, however small. Though it was only eight-thirty, she dialled Tom's number.

'Yes, please, I'd love to,' she said simply when he answered.

'That's great.'

'But I do have to go and see the solicitor and sign some papers. I should be ready soon after eleven.'

'We'll pick you up at half past.'

The day was idyllic, showing Cornwall at its best. The weather was also perfect, sunny and warm. They drove to a little cove, largely undiscovered by holiday-makers and fairly deserted. Tom had brought warm pasties, served with cold salad and a bottle of chilled wine, packed in what he called the 'Eskie'.

'Kiwi term,' he explained.

Jake hauled a large bag with a collection of buckets and spades and other beach paraphernalia, and while

Lauren and Tom lay on a rug in the shade of some rocks, he played happily in the sand some feet away.

Tom rolled over to lean on his elbows. He looked down at her. 'So, are you going to tell me about yourself?' he invited.

She tensed, not wanting to spoil the day.

'It's OK. Leave it if you'd prefer,' he said,.

'No. It's best if we talk. Clear the air.' She drew a deep breath and closed her eyes.

'There was a man. Adam. He was a year ahead of me at uni. He was very popular. Good looking. Clever. Most of the girls fancied him but for some reason he chose me. I could hardly believe my luck. We did everything together. I thought I really loved him and that he loved me. So when he asked me to marry him, I said yes. We had no money and everyone, including our parents, thought we were mad, so we did it in secret. It seemed very romantic at the time.'

She paused. 'I didn't mean it to happen, but after a few months I discovered I was pregnant. Adam was horrified. He didn't want to know. He — he wanted me to have an abortion but I — well, I couldn't do it.'

'So, what happened? Did you have the baby adopted?'

'I lost the baby. We went climbing. Adam was a leading light in the university climbing club and I went along. That's when I had the fall I told you about.' She still felt the sweep of pain and blinked away tears.

'My poor love,' Tom murmured. 'It must have been so terrible for you. And to think you climbed down that cliff the other day with all that behind you.' He put his arm around her and pulled her close. It felt wonderfully warm and comforting.

'It was a long time ago,' she whispered. 'I really should be able to forget it and move on.'

'What happened to Adam?'

'He went off on a climbing trip for

146

the summer. He was always taking risks and — well . . . ' She blinked away tears and her voice cracked a little. 'He took one risk too many. He fell and was killed.

'I just had to get on with the course. You know what it's like at med school. I worked myself into the ground — anything to try to forget. That was five years ago.'

'And hasn't there been anyone else since then?' Tom asked gently.

'Not really. If anyone gets close, I immediately back off — just as I was trying to do with you.'

'Was? Does that mean you're not any more?'

'Slip of the tongue. I admit that I'm . . . very . . . fond of you. But I need more time to get used to the idea of someone else in my life. Someone who's free to be with me.'

She tried to sound casual but her heart was pounding at his closeness, his sympathy and the fact that she was trying to sound as if he mattered less than he really did.

He kissed the top of her head and lay back on the rug. They lay side by side in silence for a few moments.

'So, your turn. Do I get your confession now? Are you going to tell me why you left New Zealand in such a hurry?'

He sighed. 'It's not a nice story but I guess you need to hear it.'

He glanced at Jake to make certain he was out of hearing range and fully occupied. Satisfied, he began.

'Tanya — that's my wife — wanted marriage from the moment we met. I think she fancied the idea of being a doctor's wife more than she fancied me. She'd been indulged by her parents and was spoiled rotten. She'd done nothing much since she left school and was only nineteen when we met. I suppose I felt lonely. I was in a strange country and though I had some good colleagues who made me welcome, I was more than happy to start a relationship.

'We got married a few months later

and she became pregnant soon after that.

'I suppose that was the start of the real problems. She couldn't cope with being a mother and having Jake — or anyone — depend on her. She expected me to take her out every evening just like before. Meals, dancing, theatre, cinema. She wanted the lifestyle she'd always known. She couldn't seem to face up to any of the responsibilities. She even went out and left Jake on his own more than once. Met friends, went shopping.

'When I discovered what she was doing, I went ballistic,' he continued, his face grim. 'From then on she became quite irrational. If the poor child cried for any reason, she shut him in his room. I also discovered she was hitting him — punishing him for the slightest thing.'

'That's terrible. Poor kid.'

'I moved out and took him with me. It was the only thing I could think of doing. She told endless lies about me to everyone, especially to her parents, to try to gain sympathy from everyone. Eventually I knew I had to leave the country. Luckily Jake was on my passport. When I got back here, I stayed with an aunt and uncle for a while. Then as soon as I saw this job advertised, I jumped at the chance. Temporary post — it seemed like the perfect answer while I work out something permanent.'

'What happened to your parents?'

'They're both dead. Dad had a heart attack and Mum got cancer soon after. I was still a student.'

'Are we ever going to build a sandcastle?' Jake demanded suddenly.

'Coming!' Tom called. 'We can finish our talk another time,' he muttered to Lauren.

'Why do grown-ups always want to talk instead of doing proper things?' the child wondered and Tom laughed.

'Proper things like building sand-castles? OK. Lead on, then, Jake.'

Lauren watched as father and son

raced down the beach to the sea. Tom dashed into the shallows and sent up clouds of spray. Jake shrieked in delight and began splashing his father. Tom grabbed the boy and upended him, threatening to drop him in the waves. The squeals rang across the beach.

'They're having fun,' said an elderly lady as she walked by. 'How old is your little boy?'

'He isn't my . . . er . . . he's six,' Lauren replied, blushing slightly.

'Lovely to see parents out playing with the kiddies. Have a nice holiday.'

'Thank you,' Lauren said with a smile. How easy it is for people to make assumptions. But they probably did look like any normal family, having a day on the beach.

She got up and kicked off her sandals and ran down to join Tom and Jake, getting herself soaked and not minding in the least.

★ ★ ★

They worked hard to build a huge sandcastle. It had a moat and turrets and Tom spent ages making a draw-bridge with water flowing underneath. Lauren made a garden with bits of seaweed and some shells. Every few minutes, she looked at Tom and they smiled tenderly at each other. There was a new closeness between them and she revelled in the pleasure of having someone close to her, someone who obviously cared.

Now she knew the reason for the rapid departure from his marriage, she felt more settled in her mind. She gave a little shudder, thinking about Jake's mother hitting him. And leaving him alone like that — It was fortunate there seemed to be no real harm done to him.

'The tide's coming in,' she called out. 'Watch you don't get swamped.'

They began digging furiously but the task was totally futile and the sea won, as ever. Sadly they walked back to their picnic spot with Jake leading the post mortem on how the castle might have been saved.

'If your patients could see you now, soaking wet and with your hair all over the place, they'd never believe you're old enough to be a proper doctor,' Tom remarked, chuckling at Lauren.

'You're not exactly the picture of medical sartorial elegance yourself,' she countered, punching him playfully on the arm.

To her horror, a sudden scream rent the air.

'Don't!'

It was Jake. 'Don't hit each other! Please don't hit my daddy.' He was almost hysterical.

'I wasn't, Jake, not really. It was just a bit of fun.' Desperately wanting to reassure him, she tried to pull him to her to hug him but he fought her off. 'Jake — '

'Don't! Don't!' he screamed.

'It's OK, Jake, Lauren was just playing,' Tom soothed. 'Like I play with you sometimes.'

The child's lip was trembling and he was crying angry tears.

'You mustn't then. Don't do it. Even if you're playing. It frightens me. I don't want to it to be like Tanya again.'

'It will never be like Tanya again, Jake, I promise you,' Tom said. 'Now, come here. Dry your eyes. It's all OK. Truly it is.'

'But I don't want Tanya again.' His little body was still shaking.

Lauren stood back. She would never have believed her simple action could cause such a problem. She wondered briefly what the boy meant about being like Tanya. Then it suddenly struck her. Not only had Tanya been abusing the child — she must have hit Tom, too, and done it in front of the child. Knowing Tom, he would never have retaliated.

Poor man, he must have suffered so much. Maybe he'd tried to deflect her blows towards himself to save the child.

'How about we call at José's ice-cream place on the way back?' she suggested, desperate to lighten the mood.

'Where's that?' Jake asked with interest, his tears beginning to dry.

'It's the place for the very best ice-creams in Cornwall.'

'What flavours do they have?'

'Name some and they'll be sure to have them.'

Once they'd exhausted the more common ideas, the conversation became very silly, with each of them vying to find the weirdest combinations possible. Laughing, they tumbled into the shop and Lauren treated them each to a huge cone. They sat on the seawall, legs swinging.

'Shame they didn't have liquorice and shepherd's pie flavour,' Tom said with a sad expression on his face and Jake giggled, his eyes wide and happy again.

All too soon, it was time to go home.

'Thank you so much. It's been a wonderful day,' Lauren said when they stopped outside her flat.

'It certainly has. I'd offer to take you out this evening but I don't have a sitter. Maybe one night next week?'

'Great,' she replied.

He leaned over and kissed her lightly on the cheek, then smiled at her.

'One step at a time you said?'

She nodded.

''Bye, Jake. Thanks for a lovely day.'

'Am I allowed to hug you?' he said, clambering out of the car. 'I know you're not s'posed to hug just anyone. But we did sleep at your house and you did buy us ice-cream, so you must be a real friend, mustn't you?'

'I hope so. And a hug would be very nice.'

She closed her eyes as she felt him press against her. Then he climbed back into the car, a smile on his face.

'You're honoured,' Tom murmured. 'He never usually allows women that close.'

She pressed a finger to her lips and touched his.

''Bye, Tom,' she whispered, watching as his car disappeared round the corner. She wondered enviously what they would be doing for the rest of the weekend.

Good Times And Bad

Lauren's impending move to the cottage was progressing well. The transfer of the property was taking far less time than she had been expecting and she had already handed in her notice for the flat. In less than two weeks, she would be in her own home.

Her excitement was infectious. Jenny and Paula were already planning a housewarming party and writing out the guest list.

'Hey, you guys — it's my house and it's very tiny,' she protested. 'This lot will never fit in — at least, not without removing a few doors.'

'That can be arranged. Come on, Lauren. This is going to be the hottest date in the calendar. We can always spill out into the garden.'

Lauren chuckled. 'You haven't seen the garden.'

'Am I missing something?' Tom asked as he joined them.

'Fear not, oh, leader. You're on the list. So's Jake. It's Lauren's housewarming — two weeks on Saturday. Put it in your diary.'

'I see.' He looked puzzled and slightly hurt, apparently, to be the last to know. They'd spent several evenings together and he was surprised she hadn't mentioned it. 'So, how long's this been arranged?'

'About half an hour.' Lauren laughed. 'Jenny heard me making arrangements with the agents and solicitor and since then she's taken over. Scary, isn't it? One person taking over your life, just like that.'

'Very scary indeed,' he said, looking her in the eye. She felt a tremor of excitement run through her, recognising the implication of his words. It was getting increasingly difficult to be alone with him.

The ringing of the telephone brought her back to reality and the rest of the group. They were still babbling excitedly about the party.

'I'll get it,' Tom said as he reached for the phone.

⋆   ⋆   ⋆

At the end of most days, Lauren had begun searching the various second-hand shops in the town. She had very few household possessions and there would be little enough money left over once she started paying her mortgage. She found a bed and wardrobe plus some other oddments, enough to start her off at least.

Once she had started, she realised the vast list of bits and pieces she was going to need, simple things like brooms and washing up bowls, saucepans and waste bins. Her hospital flat had everything supplied so she'd never needed to buy any such things. But at least she wouldn't need the expense of a removal van, she consoled herself.

Some days, Tom collected Jake after

work and they both accompanied her on her shopping trips. Most of the sales staff assumed they were a family.

'Isn't your little boy the image of his daddy?' was the usual comment.

At first Jake had corrected everyone but now he just smiled happily. It seemed that Lauren was a part of the future as far as he was concerned. She felt flattered but scared. They often ate together, too, junk food for speed and more healthy when they could be bothered to cook. They had all achieved a very happy friendship, which was fine for the present.

Though Lauren had booked a couple of days off for her house move, the second day didn't work out quite as planned. She had agreed to be on stand-by as they'd had difficulty in organising another locum. At eleven o'clock her pager buzzed.

'Can you get in right away? There's been a major accident and they're bringing some of the injured here. Truro's already full and we're the next nearest casualty department.' Jenny sounded unusually stressed for her.

'On my way,' Lauren said immediately.

It was pouring with rain as she drove to the hospital. When she arrived, the first ambulances were already pulling up outside the doors. She dashed in and grabbed a white coat.

'Where do you need me?' she asked Tom.

'There's a mother and her daughter over there. The child's stable for now but you need to look at Mum. She's on full oxygen but her breathing's a bit thready. Shout out if you need me.'

Lauren nodded and set to work. She saw that Tom was desperately trying to save someone's leg. It looked a mess and he needed every bit of his medical skill.

Several nurses had come down from the wards and the minor ops anaesthetist had come in. All non-urgent visitors to out-patient clinics and the wards had been cancelled. The ordinary transport ambulances were re-deployed to the accident site.

Lauren stabilised the woman's breathing, and when she was safe to be left, she examined the child who was fortunate to be relatively uninjured. She had their two beds pushed close together so that they could comfort each other.

The nurses were dealing with minor injuries and calling the doctors over to look at anything that concerned them. George on reception seemed to have the telephone perpetually clutched to his ear while he dealt with enquiries and people looking for relatives. He was fending off press and television reporters as well as dealing with other townspeople who were arriving with their usual string of complaints.

'See your own GP,' he was saying much more frequently than usual. 'We have a major accident emergency here. You could be waiting for anything up to twelve hours.'

There were several people lying on trolleys. Jenny directed Lauren to a young man in a business suit. He'd been given a temporary sling and his neck was restrained in a collar.

'Hello, I'm Dr Fletcher,' she began, her usual introduction.

His arm was broken. The neck collar was merely a precaution. She called a porter and issued instructions for him to be taken for an X-Ray.

'Will it take long?' the man asked. 'I'm due at a meeting.'

'I'm sorry, I can't say how long you'll be. As you can see, we're unusually busy. You'll have to forget about your meeting.'

⋆　⋆　⋆

The day wore on, the stream of casualties seemed endless. If this was just the overflow, with mostly relatively minor injuries, what on earth could they be getting at Truro?

Gradually information about the accident and how it had happened was filtering through. It had been on a three-lane section of the road. A car had been overtaking a coach, at the same time as a lorry driver decided to pass a tractor. The road was wet after the first rain in weeks and had become very slippery. Once the first impact had taken place, several cars had run into the rest, causing total chaos.

The site made it difficult for the rescue vehicles to gain access and the air ambulance was being kept busy, lifting out the worst of the injured.

The coach passengers had mostly minor injuries but there were a great many of them, all of whom needed to be checked thoroughly.

The accident site was much closer to the west of Cornwall than to Truro. Even though they had far fewer facilities at Landris, the proximity to the accident made it more practical for the lesser injured to be brought there.

'I'd like to hear what the folks who want to close us down think after all this,' Paula said grimly. 'I reckon we've more than earned our keep today.'

★ ★ ★

At seven o'clock, there were still a few patients being treated. The volunteers from the snack bar had kept everyone going with tea, coffee and sandwiches. The ladies had spent all day dashing to and fro from the local town shops to boost their supplies of bread and rolls, while the hospital kitchen had ensured that the medical staff were given meals whenever they could snatch a moment.

'No good having you all fainting with hunger,' the cheerful cook had said when she arrived with trays of hot food.

'You'll have to send us our bills later,' Lauren told her.

'To pot with the bills,' said the cook. 'If we didn't have you lot working all hours, we'd have lost any number of good souls today. Just let them complain at the Trust and they'll have me to deal with.'

The mood was temporarily lightened. By the end of the day, the staff were totally exhausted. Evening staff and bank nurses were called in and everyone who'd been working since early morning was told to go home.

Pale, drawn and unutterably weary, Lauren sat in reception trying to summon up the energy to move. After all her efforts and excitement of moving house the previous day, she'd had scarcely any sleep the night before.

'Come on. I'll drive you home,' Tom insisted, appearing at her side.

'But you've been working just as long as me . . . ' she began. 'We've all . . . '

'I don't care,' he interrupted. 'You're not safe to drive. You look done in.'

'But you need to get home to Jake,' she protested feebly.

'He's fine. I've spoken to him. Sophie's putting him to bed. She's sleeping over this week, so there's no problem.'

He took her hand and pulled her to her feet. They went out to the car park and she almost fell into the passenger seat of his car. He drove a short distance and stopped outside the fish and chip shop.

'Stay there,' he ordered and was back within moments with a delicious savoury parcel of fish and chips which he handed to her.

'Don't start before we get home — I'm ravenous,' he said with a grin.

Lauren was too weary to protest.

'Welcome to my new home,' she said as they went into the cottage. 'As you can see, it's spartan in the extreme but you can blame the sort of day we've had for that. Today was the day I was to collect the rest of the furniture.'

They sat on the floor and ate fish and chips, dripping with vinegar and salt. They washed it down with a couple of cans of lager, bought ready for the party.

Tom grinned at her. 'Dr Tom knows exactly what to prescribe for exhausted doctors. You did well today.'

'So did you. I never thought you'd save that man's leg. Not to mention all the other stuff you had to deal with.'

She reached over to touch his arm as she spoke. He caught her hand in his and pressed it to his lips.

'Now, I'm totally exhausted and need to go to bed,' she said. 'If you prefer not to drive, I can offer you a heap of cushions on the floor. I haven't got my other furniture yet so that's the best I can do.'

He yawned and nodded. 'I think I should take you up on that. You're right — I'm not safe to drive any more tonight. I'll give Sophie a ring to let her know, and if I wake early enough I'll drive home to see Jake before he realises I wasn't home all night.'

⋆　⋆　⋆

She awoke around six and staggered down to the kitchen to put some coffee on. Tom was lying in an untidy heap on the floor. He'd put the chip wrappers in the kitchen bin and made himself a nest among the cushions.

'Good morning,' he said softly, disturbed by the movement.

'Good morning. Do you want some

breakfast? Mind you, it could be difficult — I don't know where anything is.'

'Don't you have a party to organise tonight?'

Lauren's heart plummeted. 'I can't do it. After yesterday, I really can't face it. We'll have to cancel. Besides, we need to call in at the hospital today — we can't expect the weekend staff to cope with all that mayhem.'

'I must say, I do like all this 'we' talk. It makes me feel as if there's a future for us.' He smiled gently. 'Do you think there is, Lauren?'

'Yes, of course — but there's still that huge hurdle to be overcome.'

'I know. But it is a real possibility?'

'Definitely. Now, we should have some breakfast and get to the hospital.'

When she looked in the fridge, however, the last drop of milk would scarcely colour one cup of coffee, let alone moisten a bowl of cereal.

'I'm sorry. I was just about to go

shopping yesterday when my beeper went off.'

'No worries.' Tom smiled easily. 'Look, I'll see you there and once we've taken stock of what needs doing, I'll come back here and help you straighten up. I'll have to bring Jake but he can probably do a few things to help.'

'I need a lift. If you remember, you kidnapped me and brought me home — I don't live within walking distance any more.'

'OK. Change of plan. I'll go and sort Jake and call back here for you.'

He leaned forward, kissed her cheek and left. She touched the spot where she'd felt his lips and smiled.

* * *

It was relatively peaceful in the emergency department after the traumas of the previous day.

Everyone who could possibly be sent home from the wards had left. The patients who had been kept in overnight had been found beds. It had been a squeeze to fit everyone in but, as always, somehow they had managed. The man whose leg they'd been so worried about had been transferred to Truro, where they'd taken the decision to amputate. Lauren felt sad for him and for Tom, who had spent so much time and effort to help save the limb. But at least he was still alive.

'The trouble in this job is, you have to form instant relationship with patients who are very temporarily in your life and then let go just as quickly, don't you?' she mused, back at the cottage again. 'All the same I can't help wondering how he'll cope in the future.'

'There will soon be someone else for you to worry about. There always is. You often don't even know what happens in the end — like the cliff rescue man that day. I never heard what happened to him, did you?'

Lauren shook her head.

'At least most of our people went

home yesterday,' said Tom. 'Quite a different problem at Truro. Now, what are we doing about this party? Is it on or off? Do you want Jake and me as slaves for the day?'

'I suppose we could still go ahead with it,' Lauren said thoughtfully, glancing round. 'Once everything's tidied up, there's not that much left to do. Everyone was bringing something to eat and we can call at the supermarket for the shopping and more drinks. We could probably all do with something to cheer us up after yesterday.'

'Let's go for it then. Come on, Jake. We have a party to organise.'

'Will there be games and balloons? And party bags?'

'We might manage a few balloons for decoration but no party bags,' Tom replied with a grin. 'It's a grown-up do. It'll probably be pretty boring for a youngster like you. Maybe we should see if Sophie could look after you?'

'It's her day off so she can't. I'll be

OK, even it is a grown-up thing with no decent games. Or party bags. I still want to be here.'

'You can always go to bed in my spare room when you're tired. You'll have to sleep on the floor though. I haven't got a spare bed.'

'We've got one, haven't we, Daddy? We could bring that. You have to blow it up. I like sleeping on it, it's all wobbly.'

'Good idea. We'll do that. Now, to the shops.'

By eight o'clock that evening, the cottage was ready for its guests and Lauren was delighted with how it looked. Tom had bought strings of lights and fixed them up in the shrubs and trees in the little garden. Balloons hung everywhere, creating a festive air, and there was a stack of CDs at the ready.

Lauren and Tom stood in the living room and raised their glasses to each other.

'Here's to your new home,' he said. 'And the future?'

'Thanks. Yes, to the future.'

'I hope it will be a future together,' he murmured quietly.

'So do I. One day.'

'Then I might have to leave you for a while — go back to New Zealand and see Tanya.'

Lauren felt a shiver run down her back. She hadn't thought of that. She'd begun to think the divorce was already underway and it was just a matter of time till it was settled.

'You mean nothing's actually happening yet?'

'No. I was too set on getting Jake away from her. And myself. I take it you realise that Jake wasn't the only one who was suffering from her irrational behaviour?'

'I guessed. But do you really have to go back to New Zealand?'

There was no further chance to talk as the first guests began to arrive. Jenny and her husband came in carrying large plates of sausage rolls and other goodies. They were quickly followed by several of the other members of the department and soon the table was groaning under the weight of dishes.

Jake busied himself trotting round offering plates to everyone, carefully keeping his thumb on the largest sausage roll so that he could have that for himself.

Everyone had brought some little thing for the house, everything from plants and washing up brushes to coffee mugs and teaspoons. Few people talked shop, most relishing the chance to be free and relaxed.

Laughter and chatter filled the house and garden and Lauren was glad she'd gone ahead with the party after all — this was just what they all needed.

When they all finally left in the early hours, she sat on the floor, utterly exhausted, leaning against Tom.

Jake had been put to rest in his blow-up bed long ago and was fast asleep.

'Are you staying too?' Lauren asked. 'It seems a shame to disturb him.'

'I did take the liberty of bringing a sleeping bag so I can lie beside Jake,' said Tom. 'There's plenty of room — it's a double mattress.'

She awoke the next morning to hear Tom and Jake laughing merrily together. She put on her robe and tapped on the door.

''Morning. Did you sleep OK?'

'I had a great sleep!' Jake shouted as he bounced on the mattress.

'Take it easy, sport. You're going to squash all the air out,' Tom warned. 'What do you want to do today?'

'Go to the beach with you and Lauren.'

'Well, we might have to excuse Lauren. She wants to get the house straight and she probably needs a bit of a break. Some peace and quiet would be very good for her.'

'I'm tempted by the beach,' she told them. 'But you're right. I do need to get some things sorted out. I only moved in here three days ago and I haven't done anything yet. I have to find homes for all my housewarming presents.'

The pair went off soon after breakfast and Lauren enjoyed pottering around, clearing and tidying and sorting out the party debris. They'd used disposable glasses and plates so it was simply a matter of throwing things out. She was delighted with everything — her new home, the party, Tom and Jake.

* * *

'We need to talk, Lauren,' Tom said to her later in the week. 'It's OK,' he added hastily, seeing her troubled look. 'It's good news really. I've booked tickets to New Zealand. We leave next Tuesday. I'll be away for three weeks. I've managed to book a locum so you'll scarcely miss me.'

'You don't mean that.'

'Of course not. You must guarantee to miss me like crazy.' He grinned. 'And when I come back, everything should be set up for the divorce. A few weeks and it'll all be over. We can begin

178

planning the rest of our lives.'

'I will miss you, Tom. More than you realise.'

'Good. Now, back to work, woman. There are people out there needing our attention.'

'Yessir,' she said with a mock salute.

All the same, however pleased she might feel about the future prospects, she was going to miss Tom dreadfully. He had become a very important part of her life.

Doctor Nightmare

All too soon, Tuesday arrived and Tom and Jake flew back to New Zealand. Lauren felt bereft and the department seemed to have lost its dynamic force.

When the locum arrived, she felt even more desperate. Dr William Evans, 'call me Wills', was a retired doctor who wanted to earn himself enough cash to fund a holiday trip to South America. His main concern seemed to be how many days it would take him to earn enough for the deluxe hotel tour. Within a few hours, Lauren was sick of hearing about the joys of the places he planned to visit.

'Did you know that Iguassa Falls helps provide electricity to three different countries? Apparently one can take a helicopter trip and fly right over the Falls. Gives one a perspective of the dimensions. The Falls are actually larger than Niagara and probably most people haven't even heard of them.'

'Wonderful,' Lauren said wearily. 'If you could take a look at the lady in cubicle one? Her GP referred her . . . ' She gritted her teeth, thinking the next three weeks was going to be a long haul.

Dr Evans — she couldn't bring herself to call him *Wills* — proved to be as incompetent as he was garrulous. He asked for her help at the slightest excuse. She had to deal with all the most unpleasant cases and at the first sign of any trouble he absented himself on some pretext of needing to check something with the pharmacist or anyone else he could think of.

'Pain in the wotsit, isn't he?' Jenny said on more than one occasion.

'He must have paid as far as Macchu Picchu by now. Let's hope he doesn't come back.'

'Maybe someone could sacrifice him to the sun god while he's there.'

'Now, ladies, I'm sure there's work to

be done,' the dreaded Dr Evans said as he wandered back into the department. 'No time for chat.'

'I hope you found out what you needed to know?' Lauren asked as he went into the office and sat in Tom's chair.

'Sorry?'

'From the pharmacist? You couldn't look at the poor man with the impending rupture, if you remember. Was it something I could have helped with?'

'Certainly not. A technical matter. I wouldn't expect a pretty little girl like you to be troubled by such complications.'

Lauren walked out of the office, unable to trust herself to keep quiet if she stayed. Patronising old goat, she thought angrily. 'Pretty little girl' indeed. She was probably already a better doctor than he'd ever been.

'I swear I'll put something in that man's tea before I'm done,' she muttered to Paula.

'There's a chap with a rather unpleasant boil which needs lancing. Why don't you go and take a break somewhere and I'll see if our friend can deal with it?'

'Excellent. I have to go and look something up in the . . . cafeteria.'

She fled, leaving Paula to deal with Dr Evans.

Instead of the cafeteria, however, she went to visit the children's ward. Patrick, the little asthmatic boy, was back, following another severe attack. She tried to cheer him up, knowing he would be missing both of his usual doctors. Angus and the child had long been friends and Tom had stepped into the gap very well.

'So where's Dr Tom?' he asked. 'I like him. He's funny.'

'He's had to go away for a while,' Lauren replied. 'But he's coming back. Now, how are you feeling today, Patrick?'

She noted with concern that he was wheezing quite badly despite the nebuliser and wondered if he had picked up an infection.

'Let's have a listen.'

She put her stethoscope to his chest and frowned.

'What can you hear?' he asked.

'Do you want to listen?'

She put the ear pieces into his ears and he listened, giggling slightly.

'Sounds like Mum's washing machine going mad. Bump, bump, splosh, splosh. Is that bad?'

'Not too bad but I think we'll give you some tablets. That should sort you out.'

'When's Dr Tom coming back? I miss him.'

'We all miss him,' she said more truthfully than the child could possibly realise.

She was keeping her fingers crossed that there were no more emergency calls for a while. Dr Evans on a cliff rescue would be as useful as a chocolate teapot. Fortunately it was nearing the end of the holiday season so maybe there wouldn't be anything too dramatic.

As she walked back to the department, she thought once more of Tom and Jake and wondered how things were progressing. What would happen when he got back?

Dr Evans was standing by the reception desk, apparently waiting for her.

'Ah, Dr Fletcher. There's a gentleman in the treatment room. Can you see to him, please?'

She frowned. 'I need to go back to the children's ward. Isn't it something you can deal with?'

'Only a boil. I usually leave such things to my junior staff. I need to catch up on my reports.'

'But you haven't done any treatments to need reporting,' she blurted out before she could stop herself. 'Besides, I'm dealing with a child patient — I only came back to collect my notes. I'm afraid you'll have to do it yourself.'

Angrily she stormed off, determined

that the wretched man was going to do *something* to earn his fat fees. Junior staff indeed!

When she returned some time later, she met a fuming Paula in reception.

'He made me do it! Stood back and let me lance the damned boil. Poor bloke was lying there wondering what the heck was going on. I didn't have the heart to refuse him. Dr Evans just about managed to write a prescription for him but only after I'd filled in all the details. His staff always did that at his previous hospital, apparently. How long did you say Tom would be away?'

'Two more weeks.'

'Will you poison this chap, or should I?'

★ ★ ★

The days dragged on. Lauren had taken for granted the smooth working of the department when everyone pulled their weight. Having a leader, however temporary, who did nothing at all to contribute made the work levels of all of them much greater. She even took to filling in any paperwork at the reception desk to avoid sharing her own office with the man.

Even so, he would keep emerging to see what everyone was doing.

'Just making sure everything's progressing as it should. Carry on.'

If ever they were talking, he would butt in to the conversation and tell them to get back to work, in so many words.

'We're conferring about a patient,' Lauren said angrily one day.

'A conference? Then surely this should be in the office, under my direction, rather than out here where anyone passing could hear? This place is very slack. No wonder they want to close it down.'

The nurses looked at each other in alarm and Lauren positively bristled.

'We didn't come into the office because you seem to have taken if over as your own territory. As for the patient under discussion, you have neither seen him, nor shown any interest in anyone else since you came here. Where have you got to in your trip now? Reached Lima yet?'

Dr Evans looked furious.

'Step into my office please, Dr Fletcher. I will not have these unseemly brawls in my department.'

'I'll willingly step into *our* office. I only work out here to avoid having to sit near you. The way you sit tapping your fingers disturbs my concentration.'

Paula sighed. She admired Lauren for sticking up for them, but she had probably over-stepped the mark this time.

Once in the office, Dr Evans spoke in a dangerously quiet voice.

'I will not be spoken to like that. Especially by a junior. You will apologise immediately or face disciplinary action. The managers will not be pleased to learn of your rudeness and incompetence.'

'I will apologise for speaking like that

in public,' Lauren replied instantly. 'I realise I allowed you to provoke me and I did go too far. But as for incompetence, that is totally unjustified. I have done far more than my fair share of the work since you came here. You have scarcely taken on any patients and as far as I can see, all you do is fill in a few forms each day.'

'But I have the responsibility of seeing that everything runs smoothly. I don't expect to have to lance boils and carry out procedures that can easily be done by my junior staff. You will learn, Miss, that I make a bad enemy. I won't tolerate such behaviour or shoddy work.'

'Well, it's a good job you won't have to put up with us for much longer, then, isn't it? Tom will be back at the end of the week. You'll soon be able to book your trip.'

She stormed out of the office, knowing that if she stayed in his company any longer, she might be tempted to resign completely.

'Coffee?' Paula offered tentatively.

Lauren nodded. 'I might take it along to the Ladies — at least he won't follow me there. Tell him I'm anywhere you like if he asks. Honestly! I don't think I've ever been treated like this by anyone, even when I was training.'

She made her escape, wishing fervently that Tom would come back. She missed him terribly. He never seemed to be out of her thoughts. Why hadn't she heard from him? He could surely have sent an e-mail to someone or even a letter should have arrived by now. Suppose he changed his mind and never came back at all? She felt positively weepy at the thought.

With a supreme effort, she dragged herself unwillingly back to the department. There were a couple of people waiting. Knowing they wouldn't be considered sufficiently serious for Dr Evans to deal with, she picked up their details and set to work right away.

She heard the phone ringing but continued to treat her patients. A few moments later Dr Evans rushed into the treatment area.

'Dr Fletcher, I need you urgently. Leave what you're doing and come with me.'

'I'm very sorry, would you excuse me?' she said to the young man she was treating. He pulled a sympathetic face as she followed the locum.

'What is it?' she asked coldly. 'I'm in the middle of suturing a wound in my patient's leg.'

'Surely the nurses can deal with simple stitches?' he snapped. 'You have to learn to delegate.'

'This one isn't simple. It's a very nasty gash. His leg got caught in some farm machinery and the wound needs internal repairs as well as external sutures. Quite correctly, Staff Nurse called me in to deal with it.'

'Never mind about all that. We've had an emergency call. Someone's fallen out of a fishing boat. They're calling for a doctor at the scene.'

'It sounds suitably serious for you to

go then, doesn't it?' Lauren said wickedly.

'I can't possibly leave the department unattended by any senior staff member.'

'No worries. I can cope. Besides, there are other doctors — even senior ones — in the hospital today. Obviously you should go.'

Dr Evans glared at her. 'I insist you go. Hurry now.'

'You'll have to finish off my suturing then,' she shouted as she ran to grab the emergency medical bag and a yellow jacket. 'And prescribe follow-up treatment.'

The man was quite unbelievable, she thought as she ran out to the ambulance.

'What's the score?' she asked as they drove through the streets, blue light flashing. 'Someone fallen overboard or something?'

'Boat just came into Newlyn. Man got his fingers caught in the winch. They can't get him out and they're worried we may have to amputate.

Thought it would be quicker if one of you doctors was with us. No Tom today?'

'He's on leave. Dr Evans is the locum. He thought he should stay in the department. In case any more senior decisions need to be taken.'

'Do I detect a sour note in your voice?'

'What — me? Never. Sweetness and light, that's me.'

Though very badly crushed, the fisherman's fingers were saved. He was suffering from shock and was obviously in a great deal of pain. Lauren gave him a shot of morphine and covered the hand to transfer him to the hospital in the ambulance. As they drove quickly back, she spoke to him reassuringly all the way, doing her best to calm him.

'Is there anyone you'd like us to call for you?' the paramedic asked. 'I can radio ahead and get them to phone for you.'

'My wife,' the man said, groaning.

Trying to get him to think of his

phone number diverted his attention for a while and soon they were pulling into the hospital ambulance bay. They took him straight to theatre and Lauren scrubbed up. She needed to examine his hand thoroughly and take an X-ray in case there was further damage not found at the scene. The staff were waiting and the anaesthetist standing by.

'Why wasn't I called?' Dr Evans called, waltzing into the theatre.

'I thought you'd be too busy.'

'Explain the injury, silly girl.'

Lauren bit back her angry response and took a breath. This man needed urgent treatment, not time-wasting bickering.

'This is Mr Christopher. He trapped four fingers in a net winch. We managed to free them but they're badly crushed. I need to examine them closely. I'm afraid the nerves may have been severed.'

'Stand back, please. This requires the capabilities of a senior doctor, not some young thing barely out of medical school.'

There was a gasp around the room. He was totally out of order.

Lauren paled and stood back.

'Shall I assist? I'll wait till you scrub in, anyway.' She was afraid he was about to proceed without scrubbing up. Even though there was no obvious open wound, they needed to follow protocol.

He looked angrily at her but said nothing as he went into the prep room to change. Paula assisted him, concerned, as Lauren was, that he was so unfamiliar with modern routines that he would fail to comply with the current protocols.

Eventually, like some dramatic participant in a TV medical drama, he sailed into the operating theatre. The patient was already sedated and local anaesthetic had numbed his arm. Evans grasped the man's damaged hand and peered the illuminated magnifying glass.

After a few seconds, he gave his verdict.

'It all looks fine to me. There may be some slight problems with movement but I think it'll survive. Organise an X-ray in case it's broken and then arrange for it to be plastered.'

He left the room and the staff looked at each other in horror.

'Plastered? The man's a lunatic,' the anaesthetist exploded. 'If there's no damage, that's totally unnecessary.'

'What do you think?' Paula asked Lauren.

'You heard what he said. We have to follow his orders. He's the senior man present,' said Lauren. 'Get the portable X-ray machine down. If he does need the bones setting, we can do it right away, before he fully wakes up. But not plaster — that's ludicrous. We'll bind his hand as usual and keep him in obs. and see how he is tomorrow.'

She wrote up her report and left it on Dr Evans' desk. He'd left early, having an important appointment, evidently. Probably his travel agent, she thought nastily. She clutched the back of the chair, wishing it was Tom sitting here. How much longer did she have to wait?

'Oh, Tom, I wish you were here . . . I hope I haven't driven you away.'

The thought of him being with Tanya was just too awful to contemplate. She sounded like such a manipulative woman. Who could tell what she might do to keep Tom or Jake? She shuddered.

'Come back soon, Tom,' she whispered, feeling as if her heart was breaking.

A Television Debut

'Have you seen the local paper?' Jenny called almost as soon as Lauren came into the building. It was the day Tom was due back, though no-one had heard anything from him. They were all hoping his return was imminent but so far there was no sign.

Before Lauren could reply, Dr Evans walked in.

'Good morning, all. Ready for action, I trust?'

'Oh. We were expecting Dr Asprey back today.' Paula's disappointment was palpable.

'Slight delay, I gather. I'm able to continue at the helm for a few more days. Is there anything wrong?'

'No. Nothing at all. Has Tom been in touch?'

'I gather so. The powers that be have asked me to continue and continue I shall. To work, people. We have a department to run.' He went into his office and closed the door.

'I wouldn't be surprised if he isn't adding a week in the Galapagos Islands on the proceeds of this little hold-up,' Paula said sourly. 'So, haven't you heard anything from Tom? No reason given for the delay?'

'I haven't heard anything at all,' Lauren said miserably.

She couldn't believe he wasn't here. She'd been longing for this day since he'd first left and now — nothing. He hadn't come back. As each day had passed, for some reason she'd felt more and more certain that he wasn't coming back. She must simply learn to get on with her life.

'It's official!' Jenny called out, waving the paper. 'There's going to be an inquiry into the viability of keeping Landris Hospital open.'

As a babble of voices broke out, Dr Evans came out of his office.

'What on earth's going on here? It

sounds like a beer garden, not a hospital for sick people.'

'It might not be a hospital for much longer,' Jenny replied. 'Haven't you seen the paper?'

He took it and scanned the leading article.

'Doesn't surprise me,' he commented. 'This place is quite out of date. Slack behaviour from most of the staff. Nothing dramatic happening. Half the patients could be seen by their own GPs anyhow. Strikes me as sensible to redeploy staff to where they're needed. Plenty of scope for juniors in the Truro set-up. When I was working there, we were always short of people to do the basic stuff.'

'I hope you don't repeat such sentiments to the local people,' Paula retorted. 'They love and value having us here, a local facility where they can get the treatment they need without having a fifty mile round trip at least. Lots of folk living here don't even have a car. There'd be no-one to visit them when they have to stay in hospital.'

The usually calm Paula was quite agitated. She certainly wouldn't be able to travel all the way to Truro to work every day and nor would many of her colleagues.

'Admirable loyalty,' Dr Evans replied lazily. 'Now, perhaps we could get some work done? Don't we have patients waiting?'

Reluctant to leave the discussion, the group dispersed, but all day small knots of people could be seen talking urgently. Even the patients wanted to talk about the threatened closure and several of them suggested organising a petition. George came from the main reception desk to say a reporter wanted to come and interview the staff and he'd also had local radio and television calling.

'For heaven's sake, keep Dracula out of the way,' George added. 'If he sees a chance to be on TV, he'll come rushing out. And we all know his views. You should do it, Lauren. Pretty young thing like you . . . '

He was grinning as he leapt out of her way before she could flatten him.

'Seriously, you'd be good, Lauren. Well spoken. Local property owner. Well thought of by patients and colleagues.'

There was a ripple of applause from the others and Lauren blushed.

'Thanks for the vote of confidence. If you really think I should speak for us, of course I will. Everyone put your thoughts on paper and I'll compile a bit of a speech — but make sure we keep it from you-know-who,' she added.

They all went to their various posts and tried to work as normal. It was a blow to read about something so devastating in the press. It may only be a small hospital but it served a vital role and it was demoralising to feel so undervalued by officialdom.

The article had certainly provoked a response in the community. The phone rang non-stop all morning. Poor George was quite exhausted and it became obvious they needed someone to co-ordinate the calls and log the names of those people actively willing to protest. The routine calls to the hospital were completely deluged by the protesters.

The TV company arranged to visit the hospital during the afternoon and wanted to film Lauren's statement. There were also to be various interviews by the managers and other hospital trusts in the area. Miraculously, Dr Evans hadn't got wind of the excitement. As usual, he was ensconced in his office, apparently working but in reality doing his various crosswords. They'd even managed to divert his calls through the switchboard, to keep him isolated from the press.

If only Tom were here, Lauren wished for the hundredth time that day. She was beginning to feel nervous about appearing before television cameras and she knew he would have made a much better impression than she could. She longed for his tall, comforting presence.

If the locum saw her as too young, surely the world at large would feel the same way? Tom . . . She sighed and wondered yet again where he was and why he hadn't returned.

★   ★   ★

'Dr Fletcher, I need to see you immediately. In my office.' He didn't even call it *their* office any more, Lauren noted.

'Something wrong?'

'I'll say there is. We have major problems. That leg wound you were suturing the other day. There's been a development. It became infected after you sent him home and now he's back, complaining like you'd never believe. Went straight to the top. I've just been told in a memo.'

'But I didn't send him home,' she pointed out. 'I was going to keep him in overnight. I told you he needed antibiotics, possibly intravenous and then to let him go the next day if he was sufficiently stabilised. If you remember, you sent me out in the middle of the treatment. I had to go out on that emergency. I asked you to finish off.'

'Ah, yes. Now, complaint number two. The fisherman's fingers are badly infected. You missed something. You'd better go and look at him right away.'

Lauren went into the room where the fisherman lay on a trolley.

'Hello, I'm Dr Fletcher. I was part of the team who came to get you from the boat the other day. What seems to be the trouble?'

The man looked dreadful. He was flushed and blotchy-looking and his hand was a dreadful mess. It was swollen and suppurating badly, centred at the base of one of the fingers. He was shaking and in terrible pain.

She turned the hand over gently and immediately saw that there was a small puncture wound at the base of one of his fingers, unnoticed by Dr Evans or any of the rest of them.

'Darn it,' she muttered under her

breath. 'I knew I should have looked myself and not trusted that man.'

But he'd been so certain of himself that she'd gone along with his diagnosis — to a point, anyway.

In all honesty, any one of them might have missed this. The wound must have penetrated the tendon sheath on the palm side, between the base of the finger and the first crease. It had allowed some dirt in and the result was there before her.

Dr Evans came in. 'I thought I should see what you think about it. Pity you didn't follow my instructions at the time. You now have a serious problem.'

She glared at him. 'Frankly, it's a good job we didn't. If we had followed your suggestion that we plaster the hand, something we'd never do in these circumstances, he would have been in the most terrible pain from the start. He could have lost his hand. I wasn't happy about leaving him in your care anyway, but you're in charge and we're obliged to follow your instructions, which we did — apart from putting on the plaster. Poor man.'

'A word, Dr Fletcher. Outside,' Evans barked.

She followed him, laying a comforting hand on the patient before leaving him. 'I'll be right back. Don't worry — it'll be all right.'

'Your current, revised diagnosis?' Dr Evans demanded.

'I'd say he has a very nasty tendon infection. Looking at the site of the main infection, you must have missed a puncture wound. Close to the base of his finger, in the crease. We'll be lucky if he doesn't develop full blown septicaemia.'

'Probably a reasonable diagnosis. Pity you didn't see the problem at the time. I should have sent him to Truro for proper treatment in the first place. We don't have the resources here. Get someone to organise a taxi to take him there right away.'

'Forget it,' she snapped back. 'The only advantage of him going to Truro in the first place would have been that he'd have been spared your inadequacy. I shall take care of him now and I'll treat him right here.'

She ignored Dr Evans' protests and took complete charge.

'Paula? Can you come over here, please?'

She explained what she needed to the Staff Nurse, totally ignoring the locum, and went back to the patient's bedside to explain her proposed treatment.

He nodded, looking relieved. 'Thank you. I was dreading him saying I'd have to go all the way to Truro. My wife will never manage the buses and a taxi's out of the question. It's hard enough to make ends meet as it is, and with me off work for who knows how long . . . '

'Hopefully we'll soon have you on the mend. We'll start antibiotic treatment right away.'

Dr Evans was watching from the background. Once she had completed the procedure, he stepped forward.

'You haven't heard the end of this.

This is gross negligence. I think Truro is the answer. This is far more serious than we can cope with.'

'Nonsense. You may not know what to do but I do. I can certainly manage this treatment. But I don't have time to debate this now. Everyone in the theatre heard what you said at the time. I know I'm in the clear. I'm treating the patient right here and now. I will not be made a scapegoat for your own incompetence.'

'Incompetent, eh? I'm far from it, my dear. I'm a respected senior doctor. It's your word against mine — and that's no contest. I warned you I make a bad enemy. You've been totally unco-operative ever since I came here. You don't like authority, do you?

'You think you can win with your pretty smile and that's all you need. Well, in the world of serious medicine, you'll find you need something more. Experience counts for a lot and I certainly have experience, over forty years of it. I really wonder why they take on so many girls at medical school.

They always want to leave and have babies before they've even justified the training.'

Lauren took a deep calming breath.

'I think you should leave now, before I really give you a piece of my mind,' she said firmly. She was shaking. How anyone could have reached retirement age, still be considered able to hold down a job, and yet be so utterly bigoted and unreasonable . . . well!

Quickly she organised the patient's care and made him comfortable whilst waiting for the equipment she had ordered to be brought to his bedside.

'Lauren, the TV crew are here,' called Jenny. 'They're ready for you.'

'That's rotten timing. I'm so mad at that man, I'm not sure I can speak rationally.'

The reporter came and talked to her for a few moments, putting her at ease and giving her the opportunity to outline the points they wanted to raise.

'Don't be nervous,' he reassured her.

'We can edit out anything that goes wrong. Now, try to answer the question with a statement. We edit out the actual questions before transmission.'

'So you ask a question and I don't say yes or no, but say it so it makes sense?'

'You've got it. Ready?'

'As I'll ever be.'

It was nerve-racking but with her friends around to support her, she gave a good interview.

The reporter was delighted. 'You're a natural. Well done! We'll probably be back to see how the campaign progresses. Now — I just need to check the spelling of your name for the caption.'

'What's going on here?' came the angry voice of Dr Evans. 'I come out to my department and find everyone's fooling around outside. What on earth are all you people here for? Get out of the way. This is a hospital, not a circus.'

To everyone's horror, the cameraman was setting up his camera again and the presenter grabbed the mike and started towards him.

'You don't want to do this,' Lauren said, grabbing his arm. 'He's only a locum and not staying here any longer than we have to put up with him. His words have no relevance to this situation.'

'But he obviously has something to say.'

'Please — I'm begging you — don't listen,' she said desperately. 'He loves to hear himself talk but nobody else ever wants to listen.'

'OK. We've probably got enough anyhow. OK, guys. That's all.'

Lauren knew there was about to be a showdown.

'My office. Now.' Dr Evans stormed back inside the building.

'Perhaps you will explain yourself?' he barked as soon as the office door was closed behind them.

'They wanted to interview someone about the threatened closure. Someone on the staff. The others asked me to do it and I did.'

'Without my permission? I should have been asked to speak. As senior staff member in the department, it's my job to represent the hospital.'

'You are a locum and certainly cannot speak for the staff in this department,' Lauren retorted. 'As I say, I was representing all the staff — by a majority vote. The managers also spoke to represent the hospital, so all sides get their say.'

'Suppose there had been an emergency while you were cavorting around out there?'

'As senior staff member, as you're so fond of reminding us all, you should have dealt with it. Patients were hardly going to drive in past us without us noticing. Then I'd have dealt with it professionally. Like I always do.'

'Not for much longer.' His eyes narrowed dangerously. 'I'm sending a report to management. You will probably be suspended, pending an inquiry into your incompetence.'

'And just who do you think will carry

the department until Tom returns?'
Lauren exploded. 'It certainly won't be
you. You don't have the skills or the
expertise and your man management is
rubbish. As for my incompetence, if it
hadn't been for me and the others
working our socks off for the last
month, you'd have had to face an
inquiry running into any number of
unexplained deaths. Now, I take it
you'd like me to finish my shift, or
should I leave now?'

* * *

At the end of possibly the longest day
of her life, Lauren went home and sat
and let the tears come. Where was her
life going? She could be facing suspen-
sion, if the dreadful Dr Evans had his
way. The hospital was under threat of
closure anyway. This could mean the
end of everything for Landris Hospital.
Her old friend Angus was away in
America just when she needed his help
and support the most.

Worst of all, when she had finally found a man she truly believed she could love, he'd disappeared without a trace and hadn't come back when he'd said he would. He'd obviously changed his mind about her, about staying in Britain and any future they might have together. He must have made things up with Tanya.

Perhaps she should consider giving up medicine altogether — if she wasn't forced out by William Evans.

Wearily she put the television on to see if the hospital was on the news.

Not only was it on the news, it was the lead story. The camera panned across the lovely bay and finally showed a shot of the hospital from the road. It focussed on the reporter, who began his report. There were several interviews with senior management, townsfolk and then her own piece. It wasn't quite as awful as she'd expected, given her mood at the time. Perhaps the repercussions from her row with the locum had even enhanced her interview so that it represented the anger felt by the staff.

'Now,' concluded the reporter, 'we await the inquiry and the reactions of the people of Landris. If I can believe what I'm hearing on the grapevine, it will not rest here. This town will not take this threat of closure quietly.'

Just as the report ended, Lauren's phone rang.

'Well done. You saw it?'

'Thanks, Jenny. Yes, I was watching. Let's just hope it does some good.'

'You sound a bit down. What's wrong?'

'You don't want to know. I'll tell you tomorrow. I'm going to have a bath now and an early night. Thanks for ringing. Bye.'

She needed to eat something but really had no energy to cook. She took a ready meal out of the freezer. It would take about half an hour — just time for her to take a bath before it was ready.

The phone rang again, but she let the answering machine take it. She couldn't face talking to anyone.

'Lauren? Are you there?'

'Tom,' she squealed, rushing to pick up. 'Hello? Where are you?'

'Lauren, hi. Actually I'm still in New Zealand . . .'

'What? But you said . . .'

'I know. But things haven't gone as planned.'

'It's OK. I guessed you'd decided not to come back.' Though she thought her heart might break, she was trying to make it easy for him. Sound casual, she urged herself.

'Not come back? Of course I'm coming back! It's just taking longer than I expected, that's all. I can't really talk at the moment but I wanted you to know everything's fine. I'll be back after the weekend.' His voice lowered to almost a whisper. 'I love you. Got to go.'

'Oh, Tom. Dearest Tom. Thank you for phoning.'

But it was too late. He had gone. There must have been someone listening, she thought.

Just a few more days and he would be back. She tried to be pleased at the thought, but even a few more days seemed like an eternity. It had been so good to hear his voice, however briefly. And he'd said he loved her. That was enough.

Meantime, she had to continue with the daily routines and wait to see where her own future lay. Once Tom was back in charge, she would be able to face it all. No more Dr Evans. That alone made her job more viable. Whatever reports and complaints the man had made, she had still heard nothing from the managers.

She tried to avoid seeing the locum as much as possible and kept working hard. She did her ward rounds and saw old familiar faces among the new ones. The man she had been forced to leave in the middle of his treatment was now recovering in a ward.

'I'm so sorry for the way I had to leave you,' she told him. 'I obviously didn't make it clear enough what treatment you were to receive. It was a misunderstanding with Dr Evans.'

'That man's an idiot — doesn't know what he's doing. He sent me home with a couple of paracetamol! When I saw my GP, he went mad. Said I could sue the hospital for what I'd been through. Not much point though, if it's going to close. By the way, I saw you on the box last night You did really well.'

'Thanks. Let's hope it's done some good.'

★ ★ ★

At last, it was Monday. Tom was expected back that evening. She bought the ingredients to cook a meal for him, just in case he called in on his way home. She had worked hard to get the cottage more habitable and now had a proper table and chairs, sofa and armchair. Impatiently, she paced round the cottage. When the phone rang she snatched it up.

'Hello,' said a weary voice.

'Tom! At last!' Even to her own ears, the pure joy in her voice was unmistakable. 'How are you?'

'Exhausted. Jet-lagged. Home.'

'Thank heavens. I can't tell you how much I've missed you.'

'I'd like to come and see you but I don't think I can drive another inch. You wouldn't like to come here, would you? Jake's already in bed and Sophie's not coming back till tomorrow.'

'I could bring stuff round and cook supper for us both.'

'Just a sandwich will do. Unless you want anything more.'

He sounded bone weary and almost asleep on his feet. If she was a true friend, she'd leave him alone till tomorrow and let him sleep. But she couldn't wait any longer to see him.

She packed up some bread and the fillings for sandwiches and set out for his flat.

When he opened the door she stood for a moment, looking at him, remembering every little detail of his face, his hair, his body. Just looking was enough. She dropped the bag to the floor and out held her arms. He swept her close and rained kisses down on her head, her face and neck.

'Oh, Lauren, Lauren, I was beginning to forget how beautiful you are. Oh, my darling, never let me leave you for so long again. It's been torture.'

'For me, too. I've missed you so much.'

'Maybe we should go inside,' he said. 'This is the sort of welcome I'd dreamed of,' he murmured softly.

'Lauren!' shouted a voice from one of the rooms. There was a scuffling sound and Jake came flying out of his room to hug her hard.

'Hi, Jake. I've missed you so much,' she told the child.

'We went on a huge plane. It got bumpy lots of times and someone was very sick. Daddy had to help the steward with the woman. The announcement thingy asked if there was a doctor on board and he said yes. He saved her, didn't you, Dad?'

'It was only food poisoning. There were no emergency operations with coat hangers or anything dramatic like that.'

'Do you want something to eat? I've got ham and cheese and some salad in my bag.'

'Yes, please. All of that. I'm starving,' said Jake.

'Seems Jake doesn't suffer from jet-lag like normal people.' Tom grimaced. 'But then, he did sleep for ten hours on the flight.'

When Jake finally went to bed, Tom began his account of the events.

'You saw Tanya?' Lauren asked.

'Oh, yes. She was heavily into martyred, misunderstood motherhood. When I finally convinced her it was all over, she demanded to keep Jake in exchange for giving me the divorce. She said I had no proof that she'd ever hit the child and that the authorities always favoured the mother's application.' He ran his hands through his hair.

'I had some nasty moments, I can tell you. Of course her parents supported her. She is their daughter, after all. They didn't want their grandchild taken out of the country permanently. She'd fed them so many lies over the years that they were all ready to contest my claim. They believed I wasn't fit to look after a child.'

'So what convinced them?'

'Jake did. When she wasn't getting her own way, she came at me. He nearly screamed the place down. We were staying with her parents for a few days, so they could spend time with him. He got into a state far worse than the one you saw that day. Screaming out over and over that he didn't want to be near Tanya. They saw the knife and — well, that was it really.'

Lauren's heart stood still. 'Knife? What do you mean?'

'She came at me with a knife when she realised she wasn't going to get her way.'

'Oh, Tom! Were you hurt?' She felt

physically sick at the thought.

'Nothing much.' He touched his forearm instinctively. She could see nothing through his shirt.

'She needs help.'

'Don't worry. She's getting it. Her parents will see to that. So, now it's all over. The divorce will be settled quite quickly.'

'That's wonderful. Oh — I'm sorry, that sounds awful. Oh, but, Tom. I'm so happy. If only . . . ' She stopped short and a shadow crossed her face.

'What? What's wrong?'

'It's OK. You need to sleep now. I'll tell you everything tomorrow, I promise.' It was much too late to tell him of her own problems. 'Go to bed and get some sleep. You look all in.'

He nodded gratefully. 'You're right. See you in the morning. At work.'

New Lodgers For Lauren

Lauren could hardly wait to get into work. Whatever her problems with the odious, incompetent Dr Evans, she knew that the rest of the department would support her. And now that Tom was back at the helm, surely everything would be sorted out . . . wouldn't it?

She had spent a restless night, torn between wanting to be with Tom and knowing he needed to rest. There were so many things they needed to talk through.

She was certain in her own mind now. She knew where her future lay — at least on a personal level. Work was a different matter.

'Ah, Dr Fletcher.' Dr Evans came out of the office the moment he heard her voice in reception. 'These reports you left on my desk last night. They simply won't do — appalling.'

'What on earth do you mean?'

'Your spelling is atrocious and they simply do not give a detailed, accurate picture of treatment, symptoms and so forth. Far too short and scrappy. I've been meaning to mention it for several days. I can't let management think I've been allowing this sort of shoddy work to go through to the official records.

'You'll have to re-write them. State precisely what you have done, in decent grammar, and, please, check in the dictionary for the words you can't spell. By lunchtime, if you please.'

It was fortunate that he turned back into the office and shut the door. If he hadn't he would probably have been covered in shredded paper and nursing two black eyes.

'Coffee, Lauren?' offered Paula, who had witnessed the scene.

'Arsenic, preferably — for him. If Tom wasn't coming back today, I think I would have resigned anyway. I thought he'd be here by now.'

'He's phoned. He doesn't officially

take over till tomorrow but he wants to come in to catch up today. He'll be in around ten.'

'Thank heavens for small mercies. If that man thinks I'm going to rewrite those reports just because there's the odd spelling mistake or the grammar is bad, he can take a running jump. I'm going to see my patients.'

The fisherman with the hand injury was responding well.

'How are you feeling this morning, Mr Christopher?'

'Better, thanks, Doc. I owe you a lot. Who was that other doctor fella? He acted like he was the boss but he didn't seem to know what he was doing.'

'His expertise lies in other areas,' she replied tactfully.

Like holidays in South America, she thought. With any luck he'd catch something nasty in the jungle and get lost there. She wondered if they still did shrunken heads and chuckled at the thought.

She did a quick tour round the other

patients, checking that all was well, then went back to the A&E department to begin her duties there.

It was an easy enough start to the morning, with only a couple of minor injuries to deal with. All the time, she was watching the door for Tom's arrival.

★ ★ ★

When he finally arrived, her heart did a quadruple somersault. He smiled round at everyone.

'Hi, troops. I'm back.'

All around there were greetings from the staff and George stepped from behind his reception desk to shake his hand.

'You've been sorely missed, Dr Asprey. Welcome back.'

It was surprising how well thought of Tom had become in so short a time. Lauren felt absurdly proud of him and hung back slightly as the rest of them asked about the trip and Jake.

She went over to the nurses' station under the pretext of filling in forms, but she was watching Tom's every move, her eyes hungry for him.

He was walking towards her now.

'So, Dr Fletcher, how have you been getting on in my absence? I expect everything has been running with your usual calm efficiency?'

He put a hand on her shoulder and she stiffened as heat raced through her tense body. Her blood was rushing furiously, pounding through her temples.

'Lauren? Are you all right?'

To her dismay, she felt tears burning at the back of her eyes. Seeing him again last night had been almost an anti-climax. Today, all the loneliness and tension of the past weeks had suddenly descended on her. The strain of the past couple of days was also playing its part.

'Hey, love — what is it?' He turned her to him, oblivious of the watching staff.

'It's been awful — you can't imagine how bad.'

'Let's go into the office and you can tell me everything.' His eyes were soft and tender and his hands were firm but gentle as he propelled her towards the office.

Instinctively she resisted. 'Not there. He's in there.'

He looked surprised. 'It's your office, too.'

'Not any more. I'm just a pretty little thing who was let out of medical school too soon. I should concentrate on getting married and having babies, apparently.'

'Well, the last bit sounds good to me,' Tom remarked, 'but I can imagine the effect of the first part, if he really dared to say it.'

'Oh, he said it all right. And more. I'm also incompetent as a doctor, I don't treat my patients with respect and I'm negligent. Oh, and I can't spell and my grammar's rotten.'

Tom pulled her into his arms and

hugged her, kissing the top of her head as he did so.

'If you didn't look so upset, I'd think you were having me on.'

At that moment the office door opened. Tom swung round, Lauren still in his arms.

Dr Evans stood in the doorway, glaring at the sight of Tom and Lauren seemingly hugging each other.

'For goodness' sake, have you no decency, Dr Fletcher? I might have expected such conduct from a mere nurse but not a so-called qualified doctor.' He turned to Tom. 'And you are?'

'Dr Asprey. Tom. How do you do?' Tom held out a hand, still hugging Lauren with his other arm. 'Everything running smoothly? I expect you've had an easy time with this excellent team to look after everything for you.'

Evans looked like he suddenly had a bad smell under his nose.

'Ah, yes, about that. Perhaps you'd better disengage yourself from Dr

Fletcher and come into my office for a few minutes.'

'*Your* office?' Tom said pointedly.

Evans shrugged. 'Well, I suppose it's yours, strictly speaking.'

'It has always been *our* office, strictly speaking,' Tom replied smoothly, indicating Lauren. 'We'll both come in to hear what you have to say.'

'I'd prefer to make this a consultation between senior staff. It is confidential, after all.'

'I need to check on my patients,' Lauren said quietly. 'I'll catch up later.'

She went away, aware that she was about to be totally denigrated without being able to put in a word in her own defence. She was also aware, however, that she would be wise to entrust the task to Tom, who was far less likely to lose his temper than she was.

★   ★   ★

The office door remained closed for over an hour. When Tom finally emerged, his face was thunderous. He stormed through the department, not looking at anyone, and pounded straight up the stairs to the hospital manager's office. He thumped on the door but didn't wait for an answer — he simply pushed it open and went in, slamming the door shut behind him.

Jenny, finding a sudden need to visit the pharmacy on the same route, slowed outside the door. Sadly, however, it was much too thick for her to hear anything.

Lauren thought she would burst if she didn't hear something soon and took herself down to the children's ward to chat to some of her favourite patients. Their smiles of welcome always made her feel better.

When she returned to the department some time later, the office door was once more shut tight.

'Tom's in there. With the manager and Dr Evans. What's going on, do you think?' Jenny asked.

Lauren shrugged and picked up the

next patient's card.

It was a further half-hour before the door opened.

Dr Evans came out carrying a cardboard box containing his belongings with his stethoscope draped round his neck. He raised a hand to everyone watching.

'Thanks, all. Now that Dr Asprey's back, I'm no longer needed. I'll send you a postcard from Rio.'

There was no response from anyone as he walked out of the door.

'Lauren, would you please come into the office?' the manager asked and she went in at once.

'I gather things have not been going too well during Tom's absence?' he began and she shook her head. Feeling tears threatening again, she swallowed hard. This was not the time or place for stupid emotions.

'We've certainly had a few problems,' she said in a faltering voice.

Tom moved to stand behind her, which was comforting.

'Go on. I'd prefer you to speak frankly,' the manager told her.

'I'm afraid Dr Evans was unfamiliar with modern protocols. He didn't feel it was part of his job to deal with any minor emergencies.'

'So what did he do? The ward rounds? Serious emergencies? Perhaps there were few of them during his stay here?'

'There were a few but he didn't consider them sufficiently serious to merit his attendance and left them to me or one of the nurses. Oh, apart from the man from the fishing boat. Infection set in. The patient was not diagnosed or treated properly, despite the staff's protests. Dr Evans felt he knew best at the time. The patient became quite ill but he's recovering well now.'

'That would be the case of negligence Dr Evans complained about, presumably?'

'I suppose so. He wanted to send the patient to Truro without even looking at him. There's another patient with an infected leg whom Dr Evans also intended to complain about. He insisted I had to leave halfway through the treatment to answer an emergency call-out — to the fisherman, actually.'

'Ah yes. He suggested in his report that you were flustered at the work load and couldn't cope.'

Lauren's eyes flashed. 'That is so unfair. He didn't even look at the leg injury. He got Paula, our Staff Nurse, to finish it and then sent the poor man home when I had left instructions for him to be kept in at least overnight and given antibiotics. He, too, came back, threatening action after Dr Evans sent him home and suggested paracetamol as a cure. However, he's recovering now and seems satisfied with the subsequent treatment which I ordered.'

'I'm sorry you didn't see fit to make representation directly to me. Less serious is his statement that your reports are inadequate.'

Lauren shrugged. 'I've done what we always do. Admittedly we use a degree of shorthand because it saves time — patients take precedence over report writing. I don't think my spelling is as bad as he implied. Perhaps he couldn't understand the shorthand we use. Angus was always happy when he actually had time to do any more than glance through them. He always trusted us.'

'Of course. We've never seen fit to question anything. But, as it is, I'm afraid an official complaint has been made and we have to have an enquiry. Purely an internal enquiry, so there will be no publicity.'

'I hope he'll be the one being questioned,' Lauren burst out. 'He was a total waste of space! We've all been working our socks off and he's spent hours doing crosswords and planning his trip to South America.'

She paused and the manager stood up to leave.

'We'll let you know the date of the enquiry. I saw your appearance on the television news, by the way. You spoke well. You'll probably be called on again when we enter the next phase.'

'Even if I'm blacklisted as a member of staff?' she muttered unhappily.

'Don't worry. I suspect you'll be in the clear. I think we all realise that Dr Evans perhaps wasn't our best choice of locum.'

Relieved, Lauren went back to work, bringing Tom up to date on all the patients. She watched as he dealt with questions, comforted and assessed patients and, she realised, behaved exactly as a senior staff member should behave.

★　★　★

The rest of the day proved quite hectic. Following the TV coverage, many of the locals had wanted to register their protests and a working party was being set up. There were volunteers from the local community who were taking on the co-ordination of the campaign but Lauren was seen as some sort of official spokesman.

By the end of the day she felt emotionally drained and quite exhausted, so she was glad when Tom took charge.

'I'm going to pop home to see Jake and put him to bed and then we're having a take-away at your cottage,' he said. 'I'll call for it on my way over. Now, get yourself home and have a shower. Try to relax.'

'That sounds wonderful. Thanks, Tom. For everything.'

At seven-thirty, her doorbell rang. He stood there, looking unbelievably handsome in his dark blue shirt and faded jeans. He held a carrier bag and a bottle of wine.

He followed her into the kitchen and put down the bag and wine. He reached for her and drew her into his arms and kissed her.

'Oh, Lauren, I've missed you so much. It shouldn't be too long now before I'll be free. Free, just for you. For ever.'

They sat on the floor to eat in front of the mock log fire.

'How do you think Jake will take it? Us, I mean?' she wondered.

'I think he'll be delighted. Are we going to tell anyone else yet?' Tom asked.

'Not yet. Let's get our plans properly organised first.'

'By which you mean I have to finalise my divorce,' he said quietly.

'Well, yes, I suppose so. But much more, I want it to be our secret for a while. I want to gloat over having the most attractive man in Cornwall as my fiancé.'

'Only in Cornwall?'

'OK. In England.'

He frowned.

'Oh, all right. Great Britain. Northern hemisphere,' she offered. 'Anywhere in the world.'

At last he nodded his approval.

'That'll do.'

★ ★ ★

'You look very pleased with yourself this morning,' Jenny greeted her when

240

Lauren arrived at work next day. 'So, everything is fine and dandy with Dr Tom, I gather?'

'How did you know? We want to keep it a secret.'

'Then you'll have to wipe that cat-that-got-the-cream look off your face! You're positively radiant. I'm so pleased for you — but I promise I won't say a word to anyone.'

'Make sure you don't. Now, what have we got this morning?'

'What would you say if I told you Dr Evans was coming in?'

'Nothing fit for the records.' Lauren was horrified. 'Tell me you're joking?'

'I'm joking,' Jenny grinned. 'But the look of anguish was enough to dim the light shining from you for a moment. And here comes the responsible man himself. Morning, Tom. Good evening?'

So much for keeping it secret, Lauren thought as she went into the treatment area.

★　★　★

'I've got a problem,' Tom said when he saw Lauren at lunchtime. 'The landlord's given me notice. I've only just got round to opening some of my mail and the notice is effective at the end of the week. A couple of days' time, in fact.'

'But he can't do that!' she protested. 'Didn't you have a proper tenancy agreement?'

He shrugged. 'Not really. He gave me a month's notice but it arrived just after I'd gone and, as I say, I've only just read the letter.

'It was a holiday let anyway and now he wants to have the place redecorated for his daughter, who's coming back home. I asked if he'd extend my stay, but he says he can't. I just wondered . . . well, how would you feel about us moving in with you? I know it's a lot to ask and I'll understand if you say no.'

She stared at him, confused. Part of her wanted to shout *yes* but the other part was yelling *take care*.

'I'm not sure. What about Sophie? You'll still need her to look after Jake while you're at work, won't you, and there really isn't room for her to stay over.'

'Not necessary. She'd prefer to work just days now anyhow. New boyfriend, I gather. But she'd babysit whenever needed.'

She was still hesitant.

'Can I think about it?'

'Of course. If you hate the idea, I'll look for somewhere else. I just thought that, in the circumstances, it could be a solution. You have the spare room that Jake and I could share just for a short time. We could help with the finances, too.'

In theory, it seemed a sensible idea. But having Tom and Jake move in? Wasn't it rushing things? What would people think?

'How about you both come round for supper tonight, as we'd planned? We can see how staying over works out for Jake? I'm just a bit concerned that he might not like the idea.'

'Sounds fair enough. Thanks. I'd help

with the mortgage, of course, and share the bills. I certainly don't expect free accommodation . . . '

'Come on, love birds,' Jenny called out. 'Patients are waiting.' Some of the others laughed.

'It's funny how nothing remains secret for long in this place,' Lauren said with a groan.

* * *

That evening, after supper, Jake went to bed very happily in Lauren's spare room, once more ready to share the airbed with his father.

'Can I borrow your teddy again, Lauren? Unless you need him to hug yourself?'

'Sure,' Lauren said, passing over the old toy.

Once they were alone, Tom and Lauren sat together on the sofa, listening to music.

'I'm really tired,' Lauren said after a little while. 'I really need an early night. Do you mind?'

'Of course not. I'll sit and read for a while, if you don't mind.' Tom waved his book at her. 'I don't want to disturb Jake with the light.'

'You do realise everyone's going to gossip about us if you move in here?' she said.

'Aren't they gossiping already?'

'I suppose so. Still, we'll have to be prepared for a lot of teasing.'

'I take it this means you've decided you're willing to house a homeless doctor and his small son?'

She grinned. 'I suppose it does.'

'Thank you so much.'

Lauren just prayed she wasn't making a huge mistake.

It was strange to wake the next morning with someone else in the house. Jake bounced into the kitchen when she was making coffee.

'Are we having some breakfast before we go home? Have you got any Sugar Crackles, Lauren?'

'I doubt it.' Tom came into the kitchen. 'You know you're never allowed those things. Far too much sugar.'

'Grandma lets me to have them.'

'Maybe your grandma doesn't have to take you to the dentist,' Lauren suggested and glanced at Tom nervously. Goodness, this was having an instant family! She wasn't quite sure how she'd cope. She knew she wanted Tom and Jake in her life — it was just all happening much sooner than she'd expected.

'I'll need to pack tonight and begin the great clear up,' Tom told her over his mug of coffee. 'I can't believe how much we've acquired in so short a time. We'll plan on moving our belongings on Saturday morning, if that's all right with you. Give you a bit of time to sort yourself out.

'I think we might need to buy a few more pieces of furniture. Jake will need a cupboard for his clothes and he's sure to get lots more toys and stuff very soon. Shall we go and look for something on Saturday afternoon?'

'OK, fine. I'll do some food shopping

after work tonight, so at least that'll be out of the way.'

It was all beginning to feel very homey and once again Lauren wondered whether she could cope.

★   ★   ★

Instead of going straight to the supermarket after work, Lauren went for a walk down to the beach. She needed space to think. The harbour was busy as the fishing boats prepared to leave for the night's work.

She sniffed the salty air with its tang of seaweed. This was what she loved about living in Cornwall. You were never very far from the sea.

She thought about herself and Tom. They would plan the wedding when his divorce was finalised.

Though Lauren had fears, she considered this was probably natural, and on the whole she viewed the future with pleasure and a sense of wonder that it had all happened so quickly.

From the first moment they'd seen each other, there had been something very special for both of them. Theirs was a future destined to be shared. They might even have their own baby one day.

She smiled at the thought. She'd always wanted a baby, ever since the one she'd lost, and she was actually daring to think about this as part of her future. Her future with Tom.

She spent a restless evening wandering round her little cottage. They needed time to build their life. Time for Jake to get used to the changes in his own life. Poor kid. It couldn't have been easy for him.

When she woke early the next morning, however, all her doubts evaporated. Tom was everything she could ever want in a man — a friend, a partner, a colleague. She was lucky enough to have everything in one package. With Tom in her life, she knew she could achieve anything.

The Enquiry

The volunteer who'd agreed to co-ordinate the campaign against the hospital closure was waiting in reception when Lauren arrived for work the next morning.

'We've had the most amazing response from everyone,' she told Lauren excitedly. 'The announcement by the Trust has got everyone going. They're claiming that no decision has been made yet but we want to make sure our views are heard before they reach that point.'

'Quite right. So what's being planned?'

'Well, most people seem to think that a protest march is a good start. We thought a week next Sunday afternoon. That won't hold up the business traffic and alienate any of the traders in town — and we'll have a good turn-out as most people don't work on a Sunday. We're getting banners made and leaflets to distribute. Both local TV companies have agreed to cover it and also to give advance publicity.'

'That's fantastic,' Tom called out. He'd been listening to her from the office. 'Count me in — and I should think most of the rest of the department, too. I doubt there will be anyone who refuses to march. If we all wear white coats or appropriate uniform, that'll show staff solidarity.'

Everyone in the department was enthusiastic about the plans.

'What about the other departments? We should get them involved. The Day Care Unit staff, Maternity, and I'm sure local doctors and health care workers will be a part of it.'

Lauren's eyes shone to see the enthusiasm of everyone. Somehow, the crisis had brought everyone together to work as a strong team.

'I know it's a different sort of crisis than our usual in here,' Tom said to her when they returned to the office, 'but it's good to have everyone so united.'

Paula knocked on the door at that moment.

'We have a couple of patients I'd like you to look at. A rather nasty farm accident and a child who should have been taken to her GP but we're nearer, quicker and easier.'

'Another point in our favour,' Tom said with a grin. 'I wonder if they'll join us on our march?'

★   ★   ★

The Friday evening before Tom and Jake moved into her cottage, Lauren spent cleaning. She'd accumulated very little clutter of her own, having lived in the rented hospital flat for so long. In fact, she realised, she had very few truly personal things. What did that say about her? Perhaps it was simply that she'd avoided becoming too involved in anything or anyone for so long, she'd never allowed herself to collect any more baggage, physical or emotional.

This was her last evening alone, but she realised she took no pleasure in the thought. She wished Tom was here already. Surely that was a good sign? There were still a few issues they needed to sort out, however. They hadn't really discussed the future much, apart from agreeing that it lay together. How did he feel about having more children, for example?

There was so much they didn't know about each other.

Shopping for furniture the next afternoon turned into a hilarious expedition. They seemed to find nothing suitable for their needs and ended up at the DIY store buying a self-assembly kit for Jake's room. They'd measured the room carefully and found a unit that would fit. The little boy was tremendously excited at the prospect of bunk beds.

'I bags the top one, Daddy. I'm lighter than you are anyway so if it collapses, I won't be so heavy when it falls down.'

'Thank you for that vote of confidence! What makes you think it'll fall down? I'm an excellent carpenter.'

There were several units available and Jake fell in love with a bed that had a work station below it.

'It's so cool. I can do my homework on the desk and everything.'

'But we need a bed for Daddy as well,' Lauren pointed out.

'He can use the other spare room.'

Lauren hesitated. The other room was tiny and was the one she had designated as an office.

'That's a thought,' Tom said. 'But we'd need to store all the stuff somewhere. Suitcases and everything. Is there a loft?'

'Well, yes. I suppose there's space for all the stuff I'm storing in that room at the moment. But . . . '

Her voice trailed away and Tom looked worried.

'I'm sorry. We're taking over again, aren't we?' he apologised.

'I'd just thought it might be nice to

have an office,' Lauren explained. 'But it doesn't matter. Jake's right — you both need your own space. A tall man like you wouldn't be happy in a bottom bunk for long. We'll get the unit Jake wants and then another single bed for you. We'll need some sheets for both of them, too. And maybe a screwdriver or two?'

She laughed. She didn't possess any tools of any sort. This was a whole new area she needed to explore.

They bought the unit, a selection of tools that Tom thought they might need and then some bed linen. Lauren was relieved that she didn't have to pay for it all as it would have cleared out her meagre savings completely. They packed everything into Tom's large vehicle and tied the two mattresses on top of the roof.

'Good job it isn't raining,' Jake announced, 'or Daddy would have wet the beds.' He giggled at his own joke as they drove home.

The living-room was filled completely once they'd unloaded. Now all they had to do was build the thing.

'Do you actually *do* DIY?' Lauren asked.

'Not exactly — but this is so simple, anyone could do it. We have the required six-year-old child on hand, at least. He can read the instructions.'

Lauren smiled and shrugged, feeling a degree of apprehension. She knew that many people had tried and failed all these 'anyone can do it' tasks. She also knew that many an argument had ensued — not a good way to begin their new arrangements.

'I'm going to leave you two men to it,' she announced. If they were going to fall out over it, she didn't want to be a part of it.

'No worries. Have you got the screwdriver and maybe a spanner?' he asked as they unpacked the boxes.

'I might find the screwdriver but I certainly don't do spanners,' she called back.

'It's OK — there's something in the box we can use,' she heard Jake call out.

They put the single bed in the other room, as the new unit would have to be assembled in what was already called Jake's room.

She had come to terms with the plan and abandoned the idea of an office, thinking she'd get a laptop instead of a full blown computer. It would take up much less space anyhow.

There were crashes and bangs issuing from the room, plus the occasional angry mutter. Twice she went to see how they were progressing but decided against entering when she heard their voices arguing at top pitch. Instead she went down and began preparing a meal.

At seven, she ventured upstairs once more, afraid that it would be getting too late for Jake to eat before going to bed. But then, he didn't have a bed to sleep in yet!

Tom came down looking fraught.

'I think I must be traumatised by the events.'

'Come and have something to eat.

Jake will have to get to sleep before too long. We can finish building the rest of the unit tomorrow. As long as it's safe for him.'

'But where can we put it? The room's so full you can hardly move.'

'Take the packing outside and we can take it to the dump tomorrow. The rest of the pieces can lie against the wall. Jake can use his sleeping bag for tonight so we don't have to make up the bed properly.'

'I knew there was a reason for my loving you. Come here, Doc, and stop being so organised and reasonable. I don't deserve you.'

'You're right,' she said as she moved into his arms.

'I hope you two aren't going to be doing that stuff all the time,' Jake said as he stood on the stairs watching them. 'It gets very boring for someone who isn't in the hug.'

'We can soon sort that. Come here,' Lauren said, holding out her arm.

He ran over and the three stood

hugging together until he asked if it was supper time, as he was about to die of starvation.

* * *

Once they'd got over the trauma of the DIY the next day, they enjoyed the rest of the weekend. Needing some fresh air, they took a long walk along the cliffs, where the first really chilly winds of autumn whipped the colour into their cheeks.

'Is it always this cold here in winter?' Jake asked.

'This isn't winter,' Lauren told him. 'This is just early autumn. The real winter is much colder and the winds are really strong out on the cliffs.'

'It was usually pretty warm where we lived before — in New Zealand.'

'Auckland only got really cold occasionally and we lived in a very sheltered spot,' Tom put in.

'Will we get snow all the time in the winter?' Jake wanted to know.

'Not really. Cornwall stays reasonably warm once you're out of the wind. We don't get much snow here. Shall we go home now?'

They marched back down the cliff path, holding hands in a row. As they looked down on the little town below them, they saw an ambulance rushing along the road towards the hospital.

'I wonder if they could do with any help?' Tom wondered.

'It's not your duty roster till two weekends from now.'

'All the same, I don't like to think of them being short staffed . . .'

'They won't be,' Lauren reassured him. 'I can see I'm going to have to watch you,' she teased. 'You'll be in there every moment of the day if I don't.'

'Not if it means I can't have you there with me!' He grabbed her hand and pulled her close.

As always, she was filled with the now familiar surge of pleasure to be near him, touching him. She couldn't believe her luck at being with this man. And to think that she had once hesitated about having him to share her life! From now on, nearly every waking moment could be spent near him. It was a good prospect.

★   ★   ★

On Monday morning, her happiness took a plunge downwards when she received official notification of the enquiry hearing. It was to be the following Monday, the day after the protest march.

She folded the envelope and stuffed it into her pocket, as if putting it out of sight would somehow make it go away. Whatever the final outcome, the fact that someone had thought her incompetent was a blow to her pride — even if it was the useless Dr Evans.

'Come on, tell me what's wrong,' Tom said when they snatched a quick coffee between the usual Monday morning throng of patients.

'It's nothing really.'

'You're looking pretty glum for someone with nothing wrong.' He was too perceptive by half, she realised.

'I've got notification of the enquiry,' she admitted. 'Next Monday. Of all the days to choose . . . It's the day after the march, and we're always extra busy on Mondays anyway.' She spoke faster and faster as her anxiety turned to anger once more. How could that man have done this to her?

'I'll be with you, don't worry. I'll book the time off to make sure you're not on your own.'

'I only have to go upstairs . . . it's hardly a big deal. You're best holding the fort here and having a large coffee ready for me when I come out. And a brandy would be good. And maybe some valium. Or maybe I should take that before I go into the enquiry.'

The week flew by with all the activity by the townsfolk and other supporters prior to the march. There had been a great deal of press coverage and interviews with the health trust managers, all of whom denied there would be any reduction in services if the hospital was amalgamated with Truro. There were heated arguments from all parties about the difficulties that would result from the proposed changes.

By Sunday morning, there was a frenzy of feeling and phones were ringing constantly as the final preparations were made. Tom and Lauren headed the A&E contingent, with Jake helping to carry a large banner. There was a mixture of flags and banners with 'Save Landris Hospital' and 'Save Our Jobs' and other comments, all waving in the autumn sunshine.

When it was all finally assembled the procession stretched for over a mile and literally hundreds took part.

Lauren looked at Tom with shining eyes.

'Isn't it fantastic? They can't ignore this show of feeling. They have to relent.'

Even several of the local politicians

took part and agreed to lobby in Parliament for the principle of keeping small hospital units open.

'So, now we have to wait and see.' Tom felt exhausted by the end of the day and flopped down on the benches in reception.

'But we'll continue fighting to the end,' said the volunteer woman who had done so much of the secretarial work. 'It's been great to have so much support from the staff. Thank you all very much.'

'The bottom line is, there are many of our jobs at stake. Lauren and I wouldn't want to have to travel all the way to Truro to work and we certainly couldn't afford to move any closer. The property prices are much higher there than out here.'

'Oh, I didn't realise you two were married,' the woman said in surprise.

'We're not — yet. But we're planning it,' Tom announced, leaving Lauren blushing furiously.

'Congratulations. I hope it's very soon for you.'

Jake was listening to everything he possibly could and picking up snippets of many conversations.

'So, when are you getting married?' he asked his father. 'I won't have to be a bridesmaid, will I?'

'A bridesmaid?' Tom laughed. 'Not if you don't want to.'

'A girl at my school called Jane was going to be a bridesmaid at her auntie's wedding and she had to wear a pink dress.'

'We won't ever make you wear a pink dress, sport.' Tom grinned. 'It's all right, mate. Boys are never bridesmaids. You might be a page boy, but only if you like the idea.'

'Do I have any say in this?' Lauren interrupted. 'I don't remember being asked formally — or ever saying yes. Now, let's get away from all this hubbub and get home. I have a big day tomorrow and I need to prepare.'

'I'm sorry. I'd forgotten all about it. Don't worry. After today's triumph, I can't see the likes of Dr Evans causing any real problems.'

★ ★ ★

All the same, despite reassurance from everyone, Lauren spent a restless night. Eventually she went downstairs at around three o'clock and heated some milk.

She sat on the sofa, going over and over the treatment given to Mr Christopher. Could she really have done more to save the poor man from the suffering he'd experienced? It was fortunate for them all that he had now made a good recovery. She had even seen him joining in the march, so he couldn't have held too much of a grudge. His hand was still wrapped in bandages, though, so clearly he hadn't been able to work since the accident.

One of the things she dreaded most was the prospect of having to spend the morning in the same building as the man who had been the cause of all the problems. Dr Evans was to be called as a witness before her, so she might be unable to avoid him.

Wearily, she went back upstairs and slipped back into bed where she continued tossing around for the remainder of the night.

She dressed carefully next morning, choosing a neat blouse and skirt instead of her usual jeans which she normally discarded when she arrived for the green hospital scrubs.

Knowing that she looked presentable boosted her confidence as she waited for the summons upstairs.

As luck would have it, though, half an hour before she was due to go up, a call came for both doctors. There had been an accident and the victims were arriving.

Immediately she changed into scrubs, tugged on gloves and apron and waited in the ambulance bay with Tom.

'If they call me now, it's tough,' she told him. 'This is my job and it's what I'm trained to do and what I do best. Dr Evans can do his worst. My patients come first.'

'Attagirl!'

There was a ripple of applause behind her and she turned to see some of the staff. She smiled and made a clenched fist gesture in the air.

'Here they come,' called Tom.

The team rushed forward, each knowing their role. The doors of the ambulance opened and Tom stepped up to the ramp as the first trolley was wheeled out. The paramedic yelled out details as they ran into the department.

'Patient has neck injuries and his lower limbs were trapped in the car. We got him out OK but there was severe damage to legs. Airway's clear. We got a line in and gave him fluids. He arrested in the ambulance. We shocked him twice. Chest compression since then but there's only a faint pulse.'

'We're not giving up yet,' Tom hissed through gritted teeth.

The second trolley was wheeled out of the ambulance.

'This is Rachel. Six years old. Minor

abrasions and breathing difficulties. Possible chest damage. She was flung forward but held in the seat belt. Front seat passenger.'

They took the little girl into the resuscitation room, screened only by curtains from the man who they assumed was her father. Tearfully she asked where her daddy was.

'The doctor's with him now, sweetheart,' Lauren told her. 'I think we'll take you into one of the cubicles and have a good look at you. Nurse? Can we get her out of here?'

The sounds behind the curtain indicated that Tom was not doing well. He snapped out orders to the others, anxious to try everything possible to save his patient and restore a proper heart rhythm.

'Tom,' Paula said. 'We've been trying for fifteen minutes.'

'I'm not giving up yet. We can try . . . ' There was a pause.

Lauren helped push the trolley that contained the man's daughter into the next room and allowed the doors to swish behind them. She didn't want the child to hear what was being said. It was clearly a close call.

It was half an hour later that Tom emerged and his expression proved that he had been successful. Against all the odds, his patient had come round and though his injuries were serious and would mean a long stay in hospital, at least his life had been saved.

Tom always felt a natural sense of failure if he lost a patient, but this time he could feel relief and a degree of pride.

He went into the small staff room and leaned against the window to stare out into the car park. The sun was shining and people were going about their business, unaware of the drama around them and the saving of a life. It was always the same.

He drew in a deep breath and went to see how Lauren was progressing with the child.

He met Jenny in the corridor,

walking towards him with a distressed-looking woman.

'Doctor, this is Mrs Stott. Her husband and little girl were just brought in. The RTA?'

Tom tried to lighten his tension with a faint smile.

'Mrs Stott. Come into my office for a moment. Please sit down. Your husband is very seriously injured but he's holding his own. He'll need a lot more treatment which means he'll have to stay in hospital for some weeks, but unless we find internal injuries, which I doubt at this stage, he should make a complete recovery. But you'll have to work with us to keep his spirits up and support him in many ways.'

'Oh, Doctor, thank you. I was so sure you were going to give me really bad news.'

Tom smiled wearily. 'It isn't exactly good, but at least he's alive.'

'And what about Rachel? Our little girl. Where is she? Was she in the car with him? He was taking her to the dentist this morning. I work, you see, and it was easier for him to take her in the car. He moaned about it but . . . ' Her voice trailed off.

'I'll get someone to sit with you while I go and see what's happening with her. She was brought in at the same time.'

'Oh no. Please, no.'

'Is there someone who can come in here, please?' he called through the door.

One of the junior nurses arrived and he quickly explained the situation.

In the small treatment room, Lauren was still working on the little girl.

'How's she doing?' Tom asked.

'I've put in a chest drain. There was fluid building but I think I've got it. We need an X-ray. I think she may have a few cracked ribs and I need to make sure they haven't punctured the lungs. She's being very brave, aren't you, Rachel?'

The little tear-blotched face behind the oxygen mask looked up trustingly and Tom took her hand, stroking it gently.

'Your daddy's all right, Rachel. He's got a lot of things wrong with him but he's going to be all right.'

Lauren looked up at him questioningly and he nodded. It hadn't been what she was expecting. She had really believed it would be impossible to recover him.

Tom spoke again.

'I can see that Dr Lauren's looking after you very well. Would you like to see your mum? She's here, waiting to see you.'

'Mummy, Mummy!' she cried out, stifled by the mask over her face. 'Mummy, it hurts.'

'It's all right, sweetheart. I just need to fasten you up with some tape. Keep very still for me and then you can see your mummy.' Lauren finished the task and stroked the child's hair. 'There — all done for now.'

The nurse stood by the child and held her hand, making comforting sounds as the two doctors left the room.

'Will he really recover? It looked so bad in there when I left with the little girl.'

'Too soon to know really. At least Rachel's going to be OK, so that's some relief all round.'

He went to collect Mrs Stott and took her to see her daughter.

'Can I see Ted?' she asked.

'Of course, but he's resting and Rachel's asking for you now. Go and see her first.'

'But what shall I tell her about her daddy?' The woman crumpled and Tom put a comforting arm round her shoulders. 'I knew I should have taken the morning off work,' she wailed. 'I should have taken her to the wretched dentist myself. It's all my fault. I could have walked there with her and they'd never have been in the car in the first place.'

'It's no good saying that,' Tom consoled. 'There's nothing you can do to change things now. You have to be brave for your little girl. She needs you now.'

He pressed a hanky into her trembling fingers and steered her towards the treatment room. She took a deep breath and looked at him gratefully.

'Thank you, Doctor. You've been very kind.'

'That's all right. Now, are you ready to see Rachel?'

She nodded and he led her in to see her daughter.

'Gently does it. She's still very shocked.'

Tom and Lauren stepped outside the room.

'Looks like you did a good job there,' he said. 'At least the little girl will make a full recovery. Poor woman. She needs something to keep her attention focussed.'

'Which reminds me — I suppose I should get cleaned up and go up to the managers. What a waste of time! Still, if I don't put in an appearance, goodness knows what else the dreaded Dr Evans will say to blacken my character.

Suppose they believe him and I lose my job? What then?'

'You won't. Believe me. It's just a formality.'

'I hope you're right.'

*   *   *

She changed back into her blouse and skirt and went up to the manager's office. After all the efforts downstairs, this seemed somewhat irrelevant.

'I'm sorry to be late. We had a call. An accident. I was needed.'

The group of people behind the wide table were mostly strangers to her. The chairman spoke.

'Dr Fletcher. Thank you for coming. Our meeting this morning will be in two parts. The panel joining me here are all senior members of the local hospital trusts. Once we have dispensed with the unfortunate business of the formal complaint, you can return to your duties. The rest of the day is to be devoted to discussing the future of this hospital. I understand you were involved in the protests against closure?'

'Well, yes, I certainly was. I feel very strongly about the value of this hospital to the local community.' She paused, uncertain about the wisdom of continuing.

The chairman nodded. 'In view of the intense public response to the threat of closure, we decided to bring this informal part of the enquiry forward. But we'll deal with the complaint against you, first. Dr William Evans has lodged very serious charges about your competence. Do you have anything to say in your defence?'

'Perhaps Dr Evans would like to explain in front of me precisely what he thinks I did wrong?'

She glanced round the room, wondering if he had already been in to say his piece.

'Unfortunately, Dr Evans made only a written statement. He is currently out of the country. South America, I believe.'

'That would be right. The only

reason he was here in the first place was to earn enough to pay for his wretched trip. He made that very clear from the start.'

'I see. And how would you judge his fulfilment of his role as acting consultant?'

'It's difficult for me to speak frankly under the circumstances.'

'Please, Dr Fletcher, go ahead.'

'Well, without wishing to prejudice my own case, I'd say he was totally inadequate and seemed unwilling to participate in any way with the needs of the department.

'Undue pressure was placed on junior nursing staff and the more senior nurses were asked to carry out procedures way beyond their normal duties.

'On one occasion, I was called out on an emergency assist and he left the staff nurse to suture a serious wound that in my opinion required a qualified doctor's attention. He then discharged the patient without proper examination and without prescribing essential antibiotics. I'm surprised the patient didn't decide to sue the hospital trust.

'There was a further case when . . . ' she began, but the chairman held up his hand.

'I think we get the picture. And these are patients you dealt with?'

'Only initially. I was allowed only to make the initial examination. In fact, I expect they are the reasons for this enquiry. He was trying to shift the blame for his own incompetence.' She paused and took a shaky breath. 'I'm sorry. But he made me so angry.'

'And your actual reporting. He mentioned that you provided inadequate reports. He even mentioned poor grammar and spelling.' His mouth twitched slightly as he spoke.

'As if I had enough time to write anything at all,' she exploded. 'I did my very best to keep up with the paperwork, but when you become responsible for every single incident that comes into the department, I challenge anyone to write detailed descriptions of routine procedures. My patients took priority.'

'I think we all have a clearer picture now, and with the reports from Drs Asprey and Matthews, there is no doubt remaining in my mind — and I'm sure my colleagues will agree?'

He turned to the other members of the committee and mumbled something. They all nodded and the chairman continued.

'We are all in agreement. You are free to leave now and thank you for your attendance. You are, of course, completely exonerated from all the charges.'

'Oh. Well, thank you.'

The sense of relief was tempered by a feeling of anti-climax.

'Now, we need to move on. Thank you, Dr Fletcher.'

Lauren stood up and, mumbling further thanks, left the room. She half wished she could stay and be a part of the ensuing discussion. She needed to make sure they all knew just how important Landris was to its community. In fact, she hesitated and almost turned back but then she decided she might only make matters worse. It was up to the managers and nothing she could say at this stage would affect the situation.

'So,' everyone chorused as she arrived back in Casualty. 'How did it go?'

'Fine. Full pardon.'

'Yes,' shouted Jenny, raising a clenched fist in the air. 'Not that there was anything to pardon, as you put it. None of us had any doubts anyway. How was Dr Evans?'

'In South America. His written statement was perfectly spelled and grammatically correct — but he wasn't there. That was the best part of it.'

'Congratulations, Lauren. I never doubted you for a moment,' said Jenny. 'Now, I think we need to re-focus and get back to work.'

'There's just one more thing. Did you know the panel are discussing the possible closure of Landris now?' Lauren's voice shook slightly as she broke the news.

'What, already? Now?'

'Apparently. The huge show of public feeling made them bring the discussion forward.'

'And when will the decision be announced?'

'Who can tell? It's a preliminary meeting, here today.'

They all went back to their tasks, the mood suddenly subdued. Lauren may have been cleared but the future of the hospital was much less secure.

A Joyful Reunion

People were finding excuses to pass the manager's office all afternoon. There was a faint buzz of conversation through the thick doors but nobody heard a hint of any decision. Sandwiches and coffee were taken in but there were still no clues.

In the casualty department, a steady stream of patients came and went, every single one of them talking about the march and hoping they weren't about to lose the hospital.

The little girl, Rachel, had been taken to the children's ward and her mother had gone with her. Once she'd seen her husband, he was taken to the larger hospital in Truro for the extensive treatment he was going to need.

The department tried to move back to some sort of normality. Tom settled in the office to work and Lauren went on the ward rounds and caught up with her paperwork.

'It's extremely quiet in here,' said an unexpected voice from reception. 'Has everyone left?'

Lauren looked up.

'Angus,' she shouted joyfully and ran to fling her arms round her old boss. 'What on earth are you doing here? You're supposed to be in the States!'

'I heard about the chaos you'd all allowed to happen and thought I'd better get back right away — before my hospital disappeared for ever.'

'It's so good to see you,' she said. 'You look great. How've you been?'

Before he could answer, several of the nurses rushed out to see him and clustered round, asking questions nineteen to the dozen. Cups of coffee appeared and people dashed in and out of the treatment rooms, all wanting to hear what he had to say.

Lauren glanced round and saw that Tom was missing. She went to seek him out.

'Come and meet Angus. He's back,' she said excitedly.

'So I saw. I thought it best to keep out of the way. I have plenty to do in here.'

She grabbed his arm and tugged him out of his seat.

'Don't be silly. Angus wants to see you. Come on.'

Tom followed her, looking subdued.

'Hello, Angus,' he said politely, holding out a hand.

'Tom. How's it going? You managing to control this unruly bunch? I hope you're having more success than I ever did.' He put a friendly arm round the younger doctor's shoulders. 'We need to have a chat.'

'Sure. Are you back for good now? If so, I'll need to start hunting for another job.'

Lauren heard his words and grew pale. She hadn't thought of that. Angus's early return could herald the end of Tom's position. It was only a temporary appointment after all, even if it had been made for a whole year. Her

284

mind raced through the possibilities. Maybe there was some other role he could fill? He could even become a GP. They always needed good doctors in the area. The two men went into the office. Tom turned and beckoned her to join them.

'Is it OK?' she asked. 'I don't want to be in the way.'

'Of course. It affects you anyhow, so do join us,' Angus replied.

'So, why are you really here?' she asked as she closed the door behind them.

'One or two reasons, actually. Firstly the possible closure. I felt that, as senior doctor, I should put in my tuppence worth. Though I think in view of the events of yesterday and the support shown by the town, that may not be entirely necessary. I also wanted to present a statement in support of you, Lauren, as a fully competent doctor and valued friend and colleague.'

'But how did you know about it?'

'The hospital manager contacted me to see if there was any possible truth in it. As soon as I heard you'd been challenged by that old buffoon Evans, I scoffed at the whole business. Silly man. I knew him years ago and turned down several applications from him for various posts. He did try to apply for my post when I was going away. Fortunately, I persuaded the powers that be that we should advertise and so we were lucky enough to get Tom here. I gather you've been getting on well?'

Lauren blushed and Tom grinned, reaching over to take her hand.

'Yes. We're getting married. As soon as my divorce is finalised.'

'That's terrific. Great news. Congratulations, my dear. About time too. Now, I assume you were cleared anyway?' he asked.

'Yes. It all went very easily. I'd been dreading it but it was really a non-event in the end.'

'I hope my report helped.'

'It must have done. Thank you — but you didn't even know the facts.'

'Maybe not. But I do know my staff.

What you were being accused of was totally ludicrous. I knew there was more to it. With any luck, Evans will be struck off permanently.'

'So, you said there were several reasons for you being here?' Tom prompted, still looking slightly anxious, wondering what lay in store for him.

'My final reason for being here was to finalise details of my own future role. You may be interested to meet the new consultant gerontologist for West Cornwall.' Angus beamed. 'I've finally got the position I've been fighting for. We've needed someone for I don't know how long. They've finally agreed and offered me the post. I had an interview on Friday in London.'

'Oh, Angus, that's wonderful. Congratulations!' Lauren enthused.

'You're only looking so pleased because it makes Tom's position safe here,' he teased.

'That too,' she agreed. 'But it *is* something you'll be very good at and we certainly needed this appointment, whoever it turned out to be.'

'As long as we still have a hospital in the future,' Tom concluded. 'I wonder if there's any news yet?'

At that moment, his pager beeped. He picked up the phone.

'Emergency coming in. You're needed,' Paula's voice informed him.

He grimaced at Lauren. 'Got a call. It's OK, I'll take it. You chat to your friend. I'll call if I need you.'

'So, tell me all about everything,' Angus said to Lauren once they were alone. 'Tom's a good bloke. I'm very happy for you.' The two chatted on enjoying a gossip about old friends and life in the States.

★   ★   ★

The suspense hung over them for the next few days. The promised statement about the future of Landris Hospital seemed to be taking an eternity. Journalists phoned several times a day, just in case anyone had inside news.

The manager was questioned at every opportunity but he said nothing.

It was the end of the week before they all got wind of the imminent decision to be announced. Typically, it was to be on the midday news and as many staff as possible squeezed round the ward television. The air was positively electric as the headlines were read out by the presenter.

'Landris Hospital is saved by people power. A show of solidarity by hundreds of townsfolk was enough to sway the Trust's decision.' A cheer went up so loud that no-one heard a word of the rest of the news.

'Terrific.' 'Only possible decision.' 'Thank heavens.'

The words echoed round the whole hospital. Everyone wore smiles and hugged each other or patted each other on the back.

Tom took Lauren's hand and led her back to the office.

'So, it looks as though I shall be staying here after all.'

'Isn't that terrific? It just shows what can be accomplished when everyone pulls together.'

'There's more good news. I received a letter from New Zealand today. My Decree Absolute will be through on Friday of next week.'

'Oh, Tom!' She squealed in delight as she threw her arms round his neck.

'So,' he went on, 'does that mean we can make the most unnecessary announcement of the decade?'

'Is that an invitation to marry you?'

'I surely don't have to do the one knee thing, do I?'

'Yes.'

'Oh, for goodness' sake . . . ' He began to lower his tall frame between the desks in a space certainly never designed for such activities.

'What are you doing?' Lauren asked.

'The one knee thing — like you demanded.'

'Get up, you idiot.' Lauren laughed. 'I meant yes. Yes, I'll marry you — as if there was any doubt.'

Jake's Opinion

As the happy couple came out of the church, there was a crowd of friends waiting to greet them. The church had been full to bursting and the overflow were standing on the pavement. The first person Lauren saw was little Patrick, wearing a shirt and tie and with his shoes highly polished for the occasion.

Shyly he stepped forward with a silver horseshoe on a satin ribbon.

'I hope you and Dr Tom will be very happy,' he said in a well-rehearsed little voice.

'Thanks for all you've done, Doctor. He suggested this himself,' added his mum.

Lauren felt tears burning her eyes as she thanked the little boy and posed with him for a photograph.

Glancing round, she recognised several of their former patients, smiling, waving, clicking cameras and calling out their congratulations. What a lovely feeling — she hadn't fully realised just how much she and Tom meant to the people in this community.

Tom's handsome face was wreathed in smiles.

'I feel like a celebrity,' he joked, waving at the throng.

An ominous cloud slid over the sun as he spoke and Lauren looked up at the sky in dismay as the heavens suddenly opened.

'Oh, great! The one time I dress up properly!'

She and her new husband ran for the waiting car.

'We'll do photos at the hotel,' she called out of the window.

As everyone dashed for cover, Jenny took hold of Jake's hand and they climbed into the second car.

'You did very well in there,' she told him. 'Not every six-year-old could be Best Man.'

'It was easy. I only had to pass him

the ring. I'm always having to hold stuff for my dad. He's pretty hopeless, you know. Always loses his keys and everything.'

Jenny smothered a smile.

'You were pretty cool yourself,' Jake continued. 'There's nothing to all this wedding stuff, is there? I thought it was a really big deal, the way they've been going on the last few weeks. But there was just a bit of talking, a bit of singing, the ring stuff and that's about it.'

'I suppose you're right,' the Matron of Honour agreed. 'You've still got your speech to make, though.'

'S'easy. Thanks for coming. Thanks to you for being matron of thingy. Cheers with the champagne. Then we get to the games.'

'Games?'

'Well, there's always games at parties, isn't there? I know there's a disco, anyway.'

She put her arm round the child's shoulder. It had been an inspired decision to ask Jake to act as Best Man.

'Nearly there,' she told him. 'Pity about the rain, isn't it? I hope it didn't spoil Lauren's dress.'

'I told her she'd be better in jeans,' Jake said. 'But that's the trouble with grown ups — they never listen.'

THE END

A BRIDE FOR JASON

Beverley Winter

Ace reporter Jason Edwards wants to marry Carly Smith, but Carly is a career girl and their families have been feuding for years. When she takes a job with Jason's family her aim is to safeguard her livelihood by exposing their unsavoury dealings. But Jason's instincts compel him to question her motives. Will the truth allow him to overcome the obstacles and still make Carly his bride? And when Carly discovers his reasons for doubting her, can she forgive him?

SNAPSHOTS FROM THE PAST

Angela Drake

When young widow Helen meets Ed her future at last seems bright. Her newfound happiness seems complete until a terrifying new shadow falls across her life. Someone is watching her, tracking her movements and sending her chilling photographs through the post — pictures relating to her past. Soon Helen can trust no one, and when her suspicions finally fall on Ed, their relationship is shattered. But who is Helen's tormentor? And will she and Ed ever get together again?